I0788429

SILENT NIGHT TRILOGY

JOY, SILENT NIGHT & CHRISTMAS WISH

By J.E. Taylor

Silent Night Trilogy © 2023 J.E. Taylor

Cover Art by Adrijana Cernic

SILENT NIGHT TRILOGY

BOOK ONE

JOY

I'm not your normal Kringle.

Toymaking is not in my blood. Give me a bo or a sai, though, and I'm the girl who can take down practically anything.

When Santa's protector steps down from the job, the Christmas village votes for *me* to replace him. Protecting my father on Christmas eve is important business.

A serious job like this needs a serious weapon. Good thing the elves have a surprise for me.

JOY

I PACED OUTSIDE OF the workshop, my boots cutting a deep path in the snow. The elves mentioned they had something for me, but I wasn't one for surprises. You would think that being Santa's daughter would prime me for easily accepting presents, but I was not comfortable receiving gifts from anyone.

I turned sixteen a few months ago, a product of a Christmas bump, if you know what I mean. I came nine months later, on a chilly September morning. But I was not your normal Kringle. I couldn't stand wrapping and all the Christmas trappings. My cookie-baking skills were about as good as my wrapping skills, but when I stumbled upon the art of self-defense, it was as if a bright light went on inside me. I studied every martial art there was with all the zest and excitement that the elves had for creating toys.

Over the years, I mastered jujitsu and karate, and was well on my way to mastering judo and aikido, too. I was as practiced and graceful as a ninja, or at least that's what the masters who were brought in to teach me said.

But this year was different. Bernard, Santa's sleigh guard who had gotten on in age and wasn't as quick with a sword or bo, decided to retire, leaving the position of Santa's protector open.

When the elves voted for Bernard's replacement, the decision was unanimous. The entire village voted to put *me* as Santa's protection detail.

Truthfully, I was nervous. I'd only done my arts in practice and never had cause to practically apply them. Protecting Santa was serious business, and the pressure weighed on me, especially since there had been more attacks by rogue monsters in certain hemispheres over the past couple years.

No one wanted the sleigh to be robbed, or worse, Santa to get hurt. Cutting the Christmas Eve trip short was not on anyone's to-do list, especially with the world's children's happiness to consider. No one wanted them to be disappointed on Christmas morning. Particularly not because of subpar protection.

When Bernard finally came out of the shop and saw me, he grinned. The little elf's nearly balding head made his white stubble stand out even more. He rubbed his hands together with a sparkle in his eyes that made me dread whatever he was going to say. That glow only meant mischief.

"Chrissy, you are going to love, and I mean love, what we have in store for you." He held the door open and waved me inside.

I entered and my footfalls halted at the view of the entire village stuffed into the toy shop, including my parents, who looked proud and hesitant at the same time. It was such a strange look for them. I mean, pride I was used to, but that underlying worry lacing the corners of their eyes made me wonder what sort of gift I had coming.

With all eyes on me, my face flushed with heat.

Bernard took my hand and led me into the center of the room. He dropped my hand and turned, waving to a few of the younger elves who stood to the side blocking the table behind them. Sarah, an elf with platinum hair, turned and picked up something.

When she faced us, my breath stalled at the stunning scabbard in her hands and the ornate sword handle that stuck out of it. The holder was gold and silver, bedazzled with inlays of emerald and ruby, and it shone like the sun itself. The handle of the sword was equally as beautiful with the same markings as the sheath the blade was hidden inside.

Sarah walked forward as silence filtered over the room.

My focus never left that gorgeous sword as she approached. Any sort of embarrassment at being the center of attention fled with that one reveal. When Sarah handed me the sheath, I gladly took the gift.

Bernard beamed. "It was forged with Christmas magic and a pinch of starlight from the North Star itself."

I glanced at him and raised my eyebrow. I wanted to ask how one attained a pinch of starlight, but with the Winter Warlock on our side, that probably was a stupid question. I scanned the crowd and found his silver hat poking up in the back, and he winked an ancient eye at me. I gave him a smile and returned my attention to Bernard who was still talking, but I hadn't heard a thing beyond his initial explanation.

I pulled the sword out of the case, and "Joy to the World" filled the space. The sound was perfection, and it made me want to sing along with my sword. I pushed the shining steel back into the sheath and the music stopped. I giggled and pulled it out again. This time "Silent Night" played. I repeated the motion at least a dozen times, and each time a different Christmas tune rang out.

"Every famous sword has a name. What will you name yours?" my father asked.

The perfect name came to me. "Joy," I announced and pulled the blade all the way out to inspect the sharp steel.

She hummed in my hand, playing "Joy to the World" once again.

While I wasn't all that enamored with baking or making toys, Christmas music was an entirely different story. I loved it as much as I loved my martial arts, and this gift had to be the most perfect weapon for me. Even though the glistening steel was meant for death, the tunes it flawlessly played made my heart fill with the spirit of Christmas.

I sheathed the sword and swung the scabbard over my back. "Thank you." I nodded to the sea of elves. "I accept this gift with gratitude. With Joy and my fighting skills, I should be able to protect my father from any dangers as he makes his world trek tomorrow night.”

The crowd cheered.

The weight on my back felt fantastic. Natural, like this was my calling. Maybe slaying monsters wasn't such a bad career path after all. I grinned at the thought and met my father's gaze. I would protect Santa with my life, and that twinkle of pride in his eyes told me he'd have my back, too.

After all, I was his daughter, and I was destined for greater things than making toys in the North Pole. I pulled Joy out again and held her up in the air, claiming my new role with an eagerness I hadn't felt since I'd first started training in martial arts.

AFTER THE CELEBRATION, WE headed back to the main house.

“Are you ready for tomorrow?” my father asked in the quiet of our living room.

“I think so.” I held Joy across my lap, running my fingers over the ornate decorations. “This sword makes me feel...” I struggled for the words and then met his gaze. "Invincible."

He laughed.

My cheeks heated. "I know I'm not, but somehow, holding this gives me confidence and makes me want to do more than just protect you on Christmas Eve."

His head cocked to the side. "Explain."

I licked my lips and nodded to the window. "There's more out there than just the North Pole."

He slowly nodded, although his eyes became guarded as if he knew what was coming even before I did.

"I think I'm going to like slaying monsters," I said. "I mean the idea doesn't scare me. And I know there are monsters out there terrorizing people every day."

The thought of leaving home made my stomach tighten, but it also caused my skin to tingle with excitement.

My father leaned back in his seat, and his eyes flared with hurt. "You want to leave the North Pole."

It wasn't phrased as a question.

I sucked my lower lip between my teeth and shrugged.

"Let's see how tomorrow night goes, and then we can have this conversation again when you are eighteen." He stood up, ending the conversation. He gave me a peck on the cheek and headed into the kitchen to help my mother with dinner.

I blinked as his words seeped in. While my father had been hurt by my non-acknowledgement, he'd read me correctly. I couldn't see myself hanging around the North Pole for the rest of my life.

But more importantly, my father hadn't said no.

IT WAS CHRISTMAS EVE, and all the North Pole was abuzz. I stood in front of my mirror dressed in black with the sword tucked into the scabbard on my back. I pulled my honey-colored hair into a tight ponytail, smoothing it back, and then braided it so it wouldn't fly around my face while I was in the sled. I didn't need my hair obstructing my vision.

I zipped up my winter leather coat which was heavy enough to keep me warm but loose enough not to restrict my movement just in case something attacked the sleigh. My heart fluttered as I shook out the tremors in my hands. I studied my blue eyes in the looking glass, wondering if I really was up to the task.

If a monster attacked, I would have to kill it, and I had never killed anything in all my sixteen years. It was a heavy thought, but the ramifications of not taking action against an attacker meant injury or death of both my father and me.

That wasn't an option.

"I'll do what is necessary," I whispered to my image and gave myself a resolute nod before turning on my heel and heading toward the town square where the sleigh awaited.

The moment I walked out, the square went silent. My father was already waiting on the sleigh in his signature red suit. The reindeer shuffled impatiently.

My mother took one look at me and frowned. "Well, that's not very festive," she said as I approached.

I stared her down. "I'm not going to a party." I climbed up onto the seat next to my father and adjusted Joy so I could sit. "Besides, I need to be in comfortable clothing to defend the sleigh, and in black, I blend with the night." I gave her a sweet smile. "You'd rather we get home in one piece, right?"

Her cheeks blushed red, and her lips pressed together until they were almost white. "Yes. I would rather you both come home unharmed." She gave my father a peck on his cheek and blew me a kiss. "Be safe."

"Always," Santa said and snapped the reins.

The reindeer shot forward, and the momentum pushed me back in the seat. The whoosh of air tore at my hair, trying to loosen the tightly bound strands.

My father chuckled. "There's a seat belt if you'd like." He nodded toward the sash fluttering in the wind.

"I'm good." But I left my stomach on the ground, and I wasn't sure I'd get it back until we arrived home.

A chill gripped me, and I wished I had worn one of the more sensible coats. Normally, the cold didn't bother me, but between my pulse clanging in my veins and the terror of being in an open carriage high enough that if I fell, I'd plunge to my death, my ability to warm myself fled. My teeth started to chatter.

My dad gave me a side-eye and then pushed a button on the dash.

Warmth radiated from the seat, and a small stream of hot air surrounded me. My teeth stopped their incessant clattering. My shivers subsided, and I gave my father a smile of appreciation.

"What could we run into tonight?" I asked to gauge exactly where I needed to be most alert.

"Well, New Zealand used to be the home of the peryton, which considered anything flying over their domain as prey." He glanced at me with a wink. "But they haven't been seen in eons, and I heard some migrated to North America, which is a little too close for comfort if you ask me."

"But aren't they just deer with wings?"

My father let out a soft laugh. "Deer with teeth like a tiger and claws like a falcon. They are carnivores, my dear, and we are all meat." He waved at the eight reindeer pulling the sleigh. "But as I said, we haven't seen those in years."

"Oh." I glanced around at the night sky, squinting to see if anything was coming for us as my father descended onto Kiribati. Every nerve danced on my skin, burning like a shot of pure adrenaline.

After we finished the houses on the island and took off over the Pacific once again, he said, "Or the kahui-tipua which remind me a little of the yeti, but they prefer to kill their victims by blunt trauma and then eat them instead of just tearing them apart with their teeth like the abominable used to." He smiled as if all of this was a pleasant conversation topic.

"And where do we find these kahui-tipuas?"

"Most of the high snowy mountains have at least some variations of them, but New Zealand has the most vicious ones." He snapped the reins and steered us to the right toward the land of monsters.

Great. New Zealand had both flying deer and killer yeti. Noted. The buzz of my nerves kept me warm enough so my muscles didn't get stiff as we traversed the islands.

"American Samoa has Kapua, a Polynesian monster with an elongated snout, razor-like teeth, and deadly claws that can decapitate a man in one swing."

My blood chilled at yet another monster's description, and doubt ran rapid through my veins. Even with all my martial arts training, was I truly a match for these things?

My father touched my knee, and warmth radiated from his hand. I turned to look in his festive blue eyes that looked so much like the ones that had looked out from my mirror this morning.

"You've got this. Just remember, Christmas magic is all around us, and all you have to do is believe." He tapped my nose and then was off again like a wisp of smoke, flitting from rooftop to rooftop and passing out presents to the people within each home.

Watching him work was almost as intimidating as the thought of going up against any of the monsters he'd described. Fear had a dirty way of undermining my abilities, and I shook it away like an unwanted coat.

I did believe in the magic of Christmas.

I didn't dare close my eyes, but I did inhale a deep breath, taking in the saltiness of the moist air. It was so unlike the dryness of the North Pole, and it tickled my nose, but not in an unpleasant way. It cleared my head, and for the first time since we'd left home, I noticed the rich world around me.

I couldn't let the monsters take away this new sense of awe as I glanced around at my surroundings. I was going to see the world tonight, and that thought created a web of excitement that overpowered any fear, bolstering my confidence. I had mad skills, and I had Joy. The monsters didn't stand a chance.

My father returned to the sleigh and drew his brows together.

I grinned at him. "Christmas magic," I whispered and bumped my shoulder to his as he settled in the seat and snapped the reins.

"Indeed," he said as we took off again.

The rest of the evening went without a hiccup. I got to see things I had only read about in my schooling. The Great Wall of China. The Taj Mahal. Mount Everest. The great pyramids. Petra. Victoria Falls. The Colosseum. The Eiffel Tower. Big Ben. Machu Picchu. Christ the Redeemer. The Panama Canal. Chichen Itza. The Hoover Dam. The Grand Canyon. The Empire State Building. Niagara Falls. The Golden Gate Bridge. And many other places that flew by in a blink. But every single one left an impression.

The world was too big for me to waste away at the North Pole all year.

ALL WAS QUIET UNTIL we reached one of the last islands. American Samoa. It wasn't until we reached a lone hut in the heart of the jungle that I started getting that itch on the back of my spine like we were being watched.

The smile my father had sported for most of the ride disappeared as if he felt the danger, too. I undid my scabbard and stood, holding the case in my left hand, and my right gripped the handle of the sword. It vibrated against my skin.

My father started to turn to smoke to deliver gifts, but my instincts flared. I grabbed onto him, keeping him solid as I pushed him back into the seat. I spun, unsheathing Joy.

"God Rest Ye Merry Gentlemen" barreled into the quiet night, and Joy glowed in the darkness, thrumming with as much anticipation as I had running through my muscles. Shock scurried across my skin at the beast trying to sneak up behind me. It was hideous enough to peel my teeth away from my lips in disgust.

While I had seen some things in the North Pole, I wasn't prepared for the brown, hairy, four-legged beast before me. The Kapua looked like a partially transitioned werewolf from the movies, but with teeth like a shark and eyes like a dead fish. It smelled just as bad as a dead carcass.

I was surprised I didn't smell it before now with the stench it radiated. I moved my sword in a slow Z pattern. Its dark gaze followed my blade. By the time I returned to the top of the pattern, it must have decided it had had enough. The beast leapt at me.

I swung the sword as I parried, using my momentum to carry the blade faster toward the Kapua. I didn't even feel resistance as the sharp edge cut clean through the animal's neck. Glitter doused me.

I blinked the specks of gold and red and green from my eyes and stared at the headless carcass before it, too, burst into a glitter explosion. I turned to see my father covered in the same festive confetti. His mouth hung open and his eyebrows arched at the sight in his hands.

I was sure my expression was the same.

Movement on the other side of the sleigh triggered me, and I jumped through the air and brought the tip of the sword straight down on the back of another attacking beast. The blade sliced through bone and muscle while continuing to belt out the upbeat tune.

Another glitter bomb exploded, and I laughed. Joy's victims turned to Christmas glitter.

I spun the sword in my hands as I surveyed the landscape for more Kapua. That prickling sense that had me holding my father in place was gone, replaced by a calmness I couldn't describe. I wanted to join in singing with Joy, but the natives were starting to stir in the huts below. I sheathed the blade, and ringing silence filled the jungle.

If there were other Kapua out there, they must have gotten the memo and bugged out.

My father brushed off his coat and shook his head, spraying glitter over the rooftop. Then he became smoke and delivered the last of the gifts.

I ran my fingers over Joy's hilt. This truly held the power of Christmas in its steel and in its song. Just like me, Joy was not meant to waste away in the northlands while monsters roamed the Earth. As soon as I turned eighteen, I was going to find the mecca with the most monsters and go there, where I could be more useful the other three hundred and sixty-three days a year. Christmas Eve and Christmas Day were reserved for keeping Santa safe and celebrating the savior's birth with family and friends.

When my father settled back in the sleigh, he glanced at me and beamed like I had passed a particularly hard test. "I am proud of you," he said. "The first time Bernard saw one of those things, he actually messed his pants."

I couldn't imagine Bernard being scared of anything, and the picture my father drew with his words had me giggling and snorting laughter.

With a twinkle in his eyes and a grin on his face, Santa snapped the reins, and the reindeer took off like a bolt of lightning.

It was time to go home to celebrate the awaiting Christmas feast.

THE END

Thank you for reading JOY!

Continue on the next page with SILENT NIGHT.

SILENT NIGHT TRILOGY
BOOK TWO
SILENT NIGHT

Everyone thinks the Kringles only work in toy making. Nope. I slay monsters.

But when Christmas rolls around, I protect Santa's sleigh.

So, technically, on Christmas Eve, I'm his little helper.

Most of the time, we deal with a stray rogue monster or two on Christmas Eve. But this year is different. It seems the monsters have decided they want to play with Santa's reindeer and ring his bells.

If I don't put a stop to this madness, not only will Santa be their next meal, but children all over the world will wake to a Christmas that never was.

Not on my watch...

SILENT NIGHT CHAPTER 1

"**S**ANTA CLAUSE IS COMING to Town" blares from the phone in my back pocket.

Ugh. He has the worst possible timing.

I reach to answer it in the midst of going toe-to-toe with this monstrosity of a monster. The hairy bastard attacked me before I could step through the portal to home hidden at the end of this row of pristinely manicured hedges. It's as if he had been waiting for me behind the shrubs on this deserted street in the west end of New York City. My focus only shifts for a second, but it's enough to give the creature an opening.

Unfortunately, my poor phone goes flying in the air, with the voice of my father yelling, "Chrissy!"

I'm too preoccupied fending off the swipes of his claws with one of the daggers from my belt to attempt to answer my father. Or even begin to bother with the fact that I'll likely have to replace the screen yet again as I hear the thud of my phone coming face-to-face with the cold pavement.

We slowly circle, and I get a good look at this particular being when we pass under a streetlamp. He's hideous. Even more so than the Abominable Snowman. Hairy like a Bergamasco caught in a windstorm, with arched claws that could cut through flesh and bone like butter. And the thing stinks as if he just climbed out of a sewage plant.

All things considered, I would rather be with my father right now, enjoying a mug of hot chocolate and Elise's special Christmas cookies.

My father continues to call my name, his voice growing more desperate by the minute. I'm already late, and this little encounter isn't helping. The monster must sense my impatience because he lashes out.

I jump back as one of his hairy claws swings in my direction. But not far enough. His sharp appendage catches my sweater, slicing it nearly in half. Cool air tickles my bare stomach.

"Damn it," I mutter under my breath. Better the fabric than me, but this is one of my mother's favorite holiday sweaters, and now it'll end up in my rag box.

Aggravation blooms inside me, and instead of continuing to rely on my diminutive dagger to deal with this *thing* in a stealthy manner, I'm done playing around. I slide my knives back into their holders wrapped around my waist, then reach for the sword attached to my back while evading more of his deadly slashes.

Joy, my sword, puts Excalibur in the dust. After all, Joy is blessed with Christmas magic. Forged by the elves, my steel can slice through the wickedest of monsters and still hum every Christmas tune known to man when it's unsheathed.

"Joy to the World" rings out around us when I pull her from her scabbard. I grin as I swing my mighty blade. The moment it hits the beast, he explodes in a poof of red, green, and gold glitter, raining down like a ticker tape parade.

I watch as it falls to the ground, and then I return my sword to its sheath.

Silence falls over the night.

I pick up my phone and breathlessly ask, "What, Dad? And before you say anything, yes, I'm aware that I'm late."

SILENT NIGHT CHAPTER 2

I INSPECT MY RUINED sweater and sigh. I *cannot* show up at the North Pole on Christmas Eve like this. Resigned to be later than normal, I turn away from the portal and head back to my apartment a few blocks away, muttering under my breath. This year, I had conceded and worn my mother's favorite Christmas sweater under my leather jacket instead of my normal black attire, and this is the result.

A monster attacked me.

In truth, I probably would have attacked me too with the way this sweater tends to—as my mother puts it—glisten.

My parents are going to be even more upset with me than they already are. A few minutes late on Christmas Eve is one thing, but I will be hitting close to an hour or more once I finally get there, and, to top it all off, showing up in something other than the requested "family festive" Christmas sweater.

My little one-room flat in Greenwich Village is as upscale as I can afford. Monster hunting pays a decent wage, but it's rather sporadic compared to steady work, so I have to ration my money. Although I would have liked something more than a studio apartment, I just don't see the need.

If I want wide-open spaces and a grand bedroom, I can visit the North Pole.

I wade through my drawers, and my fingers fall on the black shirt I usually wear. My mother had begged me to wear something a little more festive, particularly the now mangled sweater she got me a few years back that has yet to make an appearance in public, so I resist the urge to just pull on the familiar fabric and continue my search. Most of my wardrobe consists of grays, deep blues, and black. Outside of the festive red and green sweater the monster ruined, there isn't much of a choice.

I fan through my shirts and stop on a red blouse that's similar in fit and fabric to the black. It will have to do because the rest of my choices just lead me back to the black shirt. I pull the light, silky fabric over my head. At least it'll match my father's outfit, even if it is hidden under my leather jacket.

I stop at my tree, adjusting some of the tinsel strands. My eyebrow cocks up. Maybe if I tie a little tinsel on the hilts of my knives, I'll avoid the swarming scrutiny of the elves. I do just that. With my knives dressed in tinsel and the red blouse, I at least appear a tad more festive.

Perhaps this will ease my mother's disappointment.

I let out a laugh, realizing how absolutely ridiculous I sound, even in my own head. If it were up to her, I'd be holly and jolly, settled into the North Pole "penthouse" they so kindly had expanded with the expectation that I would be living there, with them, wasting away my days, making toys and baking cookies. Now, don't get me wrong, I do love Christmas—especially in the North Pole. However, my "toys" make Rudolph's red nose look completely normal. And don't even get me started on the hockey pucks some may call cookies that are the result of my sad baking attempts.

Though, I will say my hot chocolate making skills do come close to my monster slaying abilities. And I am one of the best monster slayers in the world.

Monsters hear my name and instantly shiver with dread. Although, there was that one that sat and laughed at me when I drew Joy and "Dominic the Donkey" began blaring. But he didn't have much to say after he came face-to-face with Joy's magic touch. I agree, it wasn't her best song choice, but it made for an entertaining victory. Then there are some, like the Abominable Snowman, who turn a new leaf when given the choice between annihilation and leaving their evil behind.

Unfortunately, most meet the sharp end of my sword because monsters usually do not change their spots. Or warts. Or whatever.

I shake the thought from my head and lock up my apartment. I am way too late to drag my feet into a daydream.

I jog back to the portal, press my thumb on the side of the bushes to open it, and step through right into a snowdrift that comes to my knees. God, how I love deep snow. Although we get snowstorms in New York City, it's not the same as the silky white snow of the North Pole.

I pull my boots along one at a time and make my way through the confusing maze of snowdrifts buffering the North Pole from the rest of the world. As soon as I step out of the maze, I grin at the sight in front of me: Santa's house, *my home,* and the town surrounding it. The sleigh barn sits to the side of the house, leaving a path wide enough for the sleigh between the two buildings. Beyond our roof towers the toy factory, which stands on the far side of the courtyard placed in the center of the property. The small elf village sits beyond the toy factory, and it winds around in small, looped neighborhoods. From the sky, it looks like a giant, intricate bow.

Even with their neighborhood, all the elves choose the courtyard to congregate in. A courtyard where I had spent many years playing with other elf children and baby reindeers. Warmth coats my soul along with the prickle of Christmas magic as it seeps into my skin.

I cross to the front porch of the house, kicking the snow off my boots. Before I step inside, I take a deep breath, readying myself, and then I cross the threshold. Before I can collapse onto one of the bright chaise lounges in the entryway, elves swarm around me, all chattering about how I'm not wearing the right clothes for a sleigh ride.

We go through this every year. Every year they want me in brighter clothing, and every year I resist.

"Elise wants you to look more festive this year!" one of the elves complains as they tug at my leather coat, as if to try to strip me of my monster slaying armor.

I fend them off gently until my temper flares when they try to remove Joy. *"Enough.* I conceded to wearing red under my leather jacket instead of black this year, just for your benefit. So enough!" I slash my arms to the sides, pushing them all away.

Silence follows my outburst, and then they scatter like ants.

They want to dress me in thick layers of glitter, velvet, and fur. But I'm a Kringle. The cold doesn't bother me in the slightest. Heat, on the other hand, is another story. Ditch me in the Sahara, and I might have a real problem. But on Christmas Eve, on the sleigh, I need to blend in with the night, not be a beacon like my father with his red coat trimmed with white fur. The only thing black on him are his belt and boots.

I tilt my head back and breathe out a sigh at the scent of evergreen and cookies. My gaze lands on my parents coming out onto the upper landing, hand in hand. The way they gaze at each other melts me to the core. Their eyes sparkle, and I hope that someday I will find that same deep, faithful, and true devotion. Love like that is a once in a lifetime miracle.

My mother's gaze shifts to mine, and that sparkle fades. Her eyes fill with nervous energy. She glances at her watch, her eyes crinkling and her lips pressing into a thin line.

We are late, and it shows in every nuance of my mother's face and body.

"It's about time." My father's less than jolly voice drifts down from the upper floor. He's all decked out in his riding suit. The only myth buster from the fable told all over the world is that Santa Claus is not fat. He's as fit as an eighteen-year-old body builder, despite being well over fifteen hundred years old. The layers of the suit just make him appear...rounder.

He releases my mother's free hand and makes his way down the curving staircase. My mother follows him with her clipboard. A few stray hairs have fallen out of her normally immaculate bun.

"What happened this time?" she asks as they descend the stairs together.

I suck in my initial response to her exasperated tone. I am always a few minutes late; it's my biggest flaw. As much as I intend to get to places on time, something always sidetracks me. It's usually that I can't get a cab or the subway is running slow, but this time, it's a little darker of an excuse.

"I would have been here sooner, but I was attacked by a monster on my way to the portal."

That stops my mother midstride. Her eyes widen, and then she hurries down the stairs as if her baby girl might have gotten hurt. Don't get me wrong, I love my mother, but she dotes way too much for my liking. I guess when you suddenly have a child after being married for fifteen hundred years, you have a right to be a tad clingy.

"Are you okay?" She inspects me for any marks.

"I'm fine, Mom." I roll my eyes at my father, and his smirk says it all. *Be patient with her.* Except I've never been patient in my life. "The bastard ruined the sweater you wanted me to wear," I add as I stop her by grabbing her wrists, stilling her hands. "I'm fine, really."

Those stress lines around her mouth soften, and a smile appears. "It's good to see you, but you and your father need to get moving if you hope to deliver all those gifts by sunrise."

We hustle out back where Santa's sleigh sits all packed up and ready to go. The reindeer shuffle in place, waiting, but I notice a couple of them are slightly swaying. I glance at my father, and he has a concerned crease between his eyes as his gaze lands on the same reindeer I'm glancing at.

"Dasher, Dancer!" he calls out.

Both reindeer look at him with cockeyed smiles. Their muzzles drip with frothy cream.

"For heaven's sake, who gave them eggnog?" Santa waves at his lead reindeer as his gaze pierces the elves rushing around the sleigh.

No one answers. They stop for a moment and trade glances with one another, only to shrug before going back to the task of getting us ready to leave.

Santa shakes his head in disgust and glances at me.

"There's no time to change reindeers." My mother glances with disdain at the two drunken beasts.

Rudolph prances over with his nose glowing as bright as the Christmas lights surrounding the village. But his gait is just as unsteady as the lead reindeer, and the same frothy liquid coats his snout.

He hiccups. "I can lead," he slurs, just before tripping and falling face-first in the snow.

We wouldn't get a mile before this drunk deer crashed us into a mountaintop. At least Dasher and Dancer are still on their feet.

"No, Rudolph. You can stay here and make sure the rest of the deer are... safe," Santa says.

Christmas Eve is a prime night for the snow monsters to attack because my dad isn't here to defend our town with his potent magic. Every mile away from the North Pole weakens our defenses. And the monsters are partial to reindeer meat.

None of the other reindeer seem to be wearing an eggnog beard. Hopefully, they are able to keep Dasher and Dancer driving straight.

I glance at the elves, looking for the guilty party, but none of them pay us much attention as they prepare the sled for launch. Something about their lack of concern strikes me, and I look at my mother.

Her eyes are hard as she scans the elves, and I can't help the worry coursing through me. When her gaze meets mine, I give her a nod. She knows I will keep my father safe, and with two drunken reindeer, it might mean being strapped into a sleigh gone wild. Although I do fight monsters for a living, driving an out-of-control sled leaves me antsy.

"Come on, Chrissy. Let's get this show on the road." Dad claps me on the back and leads us to the sleigh. He gives my mother a lingering kiss that makes my cheeks heat to watch, so I look away. "Stay safe," he says, like he always does.

"You, too," she replies. But instead of the usual excitement that goes along with Christmas, there is worry in her eyes that sends a shiver up my spine. She meets my gaze and blows me a kiss.

I catch it in my hand and return one back at her.

My stomach flutters in warning, and every cell in my body vibrates. An uneasy nervousness flushes my skin, and I sense a hard night coming.

SILENT NIGHT CHAPTER 3

TAKEOFF IS A BIT rough, but after we rise into the air, the turbulence caused by the wobbling of Dasher and Dancer smooths out. We head to the portal that takes us over the Pacific Ocean near the Christmas Islands, where we always start our travels, and the plan is to move west across the globe.

Usually, we break through the barrier just as the sun is setting, but tonight, darkness has already shrouded the land. A testament to just how late we are and how sluggish the reindeer seem to be tonight.

The first few islands bring about nothing that alarms me, and I find myself relaxing in the seat next to my father as we bound from hut to hut on these tiny remote islands. I cannot help but be amused at the transition from an almost microscopic speck in the night sky, to the fully fledged sleigh as we blast through the time zones.

As we start our descent into Upper Hutt, New Zealand, movement to my right catches my eye. I stare out into the clouds, confused. What looks like a winged reindeer barrels at us at a speed much faster than we're moving.

Dad lands the sleigh on the next roof, but before he can get out with his sack, that flying deer crashes into Blitzen, nearly knocking the entire sleigh off the house. Santa goes flying, and I grab for him, catching the hem of his jacket and hauling him back into the teetering sleigh.

Blitzen barks in pain as the peryton attempts to pull his antlers from the reindeer's shoulder so he can attack yet again. The beast hisses as he pulls, like he's just as spitting mad as I am.

I make sure my father is stable on his feet before I let go of him and reach for Joy. Unsheathing it makes "Jingle Bell Rock" echo off the rooftop. I leap in the air, bringing the point down through the peryton's neck. The sickening snap of its spine is muted by the spontaneous combustion into that red, green, and gold glitter that my sword's typical kill shot makes.

Just as I slide Joy back into her holster, the neighbor's front porch light flips on.

"Shit! Dad, go dark!"

My father presses the only non-festive button on the sleigh, and we become invisible to the human eye. Just in time, too, because the neighbor's door swings open, and a gentleman comes out with his forehead scrunched in confusion. He looks this way and that, searching the darkness for the source of the Christmas music that had just blasted through the neighborhood. He shakes his head and steps back inside his house. With the slam of the front door and the porch light flicking off, we are in the clear.

I wave my father toward the chimney, reminding him of why we're here, and he swipes his finger across his nose before turning into a magical line of sparks that make their way down the chimney.

Christmas magic is both powerful and beautiful at the same time, and tonight is the only night that it is infused in my bones and not just in the steel of my sword. I can wield it into a protective shield through song and form it into anything, as long as I believe.

If my father ever retires, I might inherit the magic he harbors, but that means I would need to retire from monster hunting, and I don't want to do that. No matter how magical this night is, I thrive on the chase as well as ridding the earth of things children and adults alike fear.

Toy making and distribution simply don't give me that same rush.

After my father disappears, I spin toward Blitzen, sheathing my sword and silencing its chirpy melody. I gently stroke my palms across his wounds, pushing my temporary Christmas magic outward and wishing for his injuries to mend.

He whines under my healing touch.

"I know it hurts," I murmur softly in his ear. "But you will be better than before." My hand brushes the last of the cuts, making them disappear as if they were never there.

My father climbs back into the sleigh, and I settle into the seat beside him.

"It has been a very long time since I've seen a peryton." He mushes the reindeer to the next stop as he shakes his head with disbelief. "I thought they were extinct."

"Well, the monster that attacked me in New York hasn't been seen in decades, either," I say as he secures his bag. "I don't even know what the name for that one is, but I can tell you that in all my discussions with other monster hunters, that thing has never been described."

Santa pauses and looks at me before glancing at the sky around us. He nibbles on his bottom lip as if there's something more I should know about, but as soon as that doubt glazes his eyes, it dissipates, and he turns to do his job. "Keep vigilant." He tosses those words over his shoulder at me as if I'm anything but attentive on these Christmas treks.

I nearly laugh, but I'm not sure if that lob was meant for me or the reindeer. Everyone besides Dasher and Dancer are looking out at the night sky, their muscles twitching under their heavy hides as if expecting another attack.

Hell, my muscles are tight, too, and my hands ache to hold Joy. But Dad prefers silence on this night as opposed to filling the eve with music. The less attention drawn to the sky, the more mysterious Christmas morning is for the children.

And this night is all about bringing children the wonder of the season.

SILENT NIGHT CHAPTER 4

IT TAKES US A few more portals going north to south and back before we're over Russia, with Moscow looming in the distance. The clock on the dashboard clicks off the minutes left, and we both stare at it as the seconds slip away. With our lead reindeer still reeling from the eggnog, we are still woefully behind.

At this pace, we'll be hitting Hawaii and Midway when the sky was on the verge of daybreak, which isn't ideal, and it means we'll be late for Mom's Christmas dinner.

Santa mutters under his breath, pulling my eyes to him. I follow his line of sight, and it feels as if an electric zap runs through me. In the distance, more winged creatures dance across the moon. I count at least six beasts before they fade into the night sky beyond the moon's illumination. Even at this distance, I can tell they are large enough to do damage.

"Crap." I jump to my feet and reach for my sword.

"Chrissy!" Dad exclaims before I can unsheathe the music maker. His pained gaze finds mine.

I don't care that he wants silence on our travels. I need to defend this sleigh. I pull Joy from her scabbard, and she belts out "We Wish You a Merry Christmas."

"This is my job for the other three hundred and sixty-three days of the year." I smile at his questioning glare. Turning away, I debate on where I should launch my attack. If I'm too close to Santa, I run the risk of slicing him with Joy. And if I cut deep enough, that will ruin Christmas for the rest of the globe.

But if I'm too far away, he could get attacked. That thought layers a cold chill over my skin.

He cannot be defenseless.

I pull out two daggers and flip them so I'm holding the sharp ends before extending them to my father. "If they come near you, swipe them with these."

He eyes the approaching monsters and takes the weapons without question. Santa may be jolly, but he is no pushover. After all, he was the one who taught me a lot of defensive moves before I left the North Pole.

He made me into the badass I am today.

I shake the thought away and refocus on our current situation. My gaze lands on the white fur lining his red coat. "Hopefully you won't get blood on your fur."

"I'm sure it will be just fine," he retorts, but his eyes betray him.

It's as if he has inside knowledge that I don't. I'll have to have a serious talk with him after these beasts are taken care of.

But for now, whether I can protect the reindeer and Santa at the same time all depends on my positioning. I move to the front of the sleigh, balancing between the polished sleigh and the harness bar that connects all the reindeer.

With a quick glance at the sky, I calculate how long I have before they reach us. Leaving the deer vulnerable could be a problem. Hell, having two drunk deer leading us *is* a problem, but it isn't something I can solve at the moment. Though they should see the ramifications of their little eggnog adventures, I don't want them to be harmed.

I glance at our situation, flying above the dark, deserted ground below us. Something in my brain clicks. The reindeer are exposed on the underside should there be an attack from below.

There is only one way to handle this. I start singing along with Joy, building up my protective magic. It swells inside me. Unfortunately, my ability to direct it is limited, and when I direct it to fly underneath the reindeer, only a portion of the team is covered. Six of the eight reindeer look as if they are running on a golden path that remains steady underneath them. However, the last two, Donner and Blitzen, are still vulnerable.

If some poor, unfortunate monster decides to gut one of the front reindeer, they won't get very far. My protective layer is the equivalent of a kill shot with Joy.

That golden barrier will stay in place for as long as I keep singing.

My father's deep, baritone voice joins mine, and his magic swells, connecting to my protective barrier and extending it underneath the sleigh itself. Of course, Santa's voice is like listening to the angels sing, and the reindeer respond by gliding through the air like a hot knife through my mother's sweet rolls.

Joy transitions to "God Rest Ye Merry Gentlemen." The staccato beat matches my thundering pulse as the winged creatures approach.

The sleigh dips, as if aiming for a landing on another roof.

"We cannot bring these beasts into a human dwelling!" My father breaks his song, leaving the sleigh vulnerable. "Circle higher in the sky until we dispatch these things." He ties off the reins to the controls and bursts back into song, helping fortify the barrier below.

I squint, trying to figure out what they are, but a cloud drifts over the moon, blocking our ability to identify them. However, they are close enough now for me to catch a red reflection where I think their eyes are.

"What are they?" I whisper between verses.

"Gargoyles," Santa hisses as he takes another breath and returns to the melody.

Gargoyles?

What the actual hell?

That's a beast I've never fought. They are inherent protectors, not mindless attack monkeys. And the ones I've met certainly did not have evil red eyes. Another fact surfaces in my mind, making my eyes widen.

Gargoyles only attack under command.

Which means someone is orchestrating these attacks.

I swallow hard and glance back at my father. Who would want to harm Santa Claus?

Who would want to harm *my father*?

The burn of anger starts in my toes and travels up my body into my hands, changing the tune Joy is casting out. "You're a Mean One, Mr. Grinch" comes sailing out of my mouth as if I'm hurling insults at the gargoyles.

I will find out who led this attack, and I will lay waste to every last one of them.

It's as if the gargoyles sense my mood shifting into full battle mode. They plummet toward us like cannon blasts in the sky. I hold Joy at the ready, and my father has both blades poised in his hands. We continue to sing to protect the reindeer. The magical glow flares around Joy as they attack.

I swing, spin, and dance on the backs of the reindeer as glitter fills the air around us. My father grunts from behind me, and I leap onto the sleigh to fillet the gargoyle that has my father's arm in his mouth.

There is no time to inspect his wounds. A deer screams. I spin back and sprint across the joist between the reindeer, swinging Joy around as if it's a baton. With a thrust, I take out the creature on Dancer's back as the end of the song flows from my mouth.

The tune Joy decides on next is "Do They Know It's Christmas?" and the irony is not lost on me as I strike down another gargoyle.

"Where are they coming from?" I shout between hoarse verses.

When no answer comes from behind me, I turn, and horror fills me at the sight of two gargoyles tearing into my father's coat. I want to launch Joy at them, but it would only serve to harm my father more than he was already hurt. Instead, I run and swing my blade, slicing into the two.

But it isn't a kill shot, and they turn their sights on me. The moment they release my father from their monstrous hands, I cut them down with a battle cry that shakes the night around us.

I can hardly breathe, unable to fully grasp the horror of what they've done to my father. His eyes seem to lose their frantic quality as his gaze finds mine. He offers me a warm smile that soon turns to a grimace as he tries to move.

"Don't," I chide, laying Joy down next to me on the seat. She hums quietly, and I reach to loosen my father's belt so I can see the damage the creatures caused. His suit is all but ruined and underneath, his blood flows at an alarming pace.

"Chrissy," he gasps as the reindeer descend onto a nearby roof, the movement jostling both of us.

I don't think the reindeer understand how dire the situation is. Not with them waiting so patiently for Santa to do his job.

But Santa is not in any condition to spread Christmas cheer.

When his eyes slip closed, my heart plunges into a free fall.

SILENT NIGHT CHAPTER 5

IT'S CHRISTMAS. A TIME where miracles come true.

I blink back the sudden swell of tears blurring my vision and slide Joy into her holder. A deathly silence flows over us, and I rub my hands together, calling on every last ounce of my Christmas magic.

I need more than just the spirit of Christmas to bring my father back from the brink. I need a miracle from God above.

I close my eyes, press my hands against Santa's shredded skin, and let "Silent Night" fall from my lips. I put my entire soul into the song and push all my healing Christmas magic into him.

The reindeer's voices join in with me, singing. The noise drifts into the night sky like a glorious prayer. Lights all over the neighborhood we're in start snapping on, creating a soft glow on the street below us. When warmth flows through me, I glance to the light radiating from the heavens above. My hands tingle with the power of the Lord as it flows into my father's form, mending the cuts and stanching the outflow of blood.

As the final note drifts on the air, Santa inhales sharply, as if waking from a nightmare. His gaze jumps to mine and then down at my hands splayed out on his chest before snapping back up in wide surprise.

"You…brought me back?" he asks.

Exhaustion ripples through me, but I can't help but smile down at him and nod. I lean back on my haunches and pull my blood-covered hands away from him, wiping them on my thighs. "Christmas magic," I whisper, acutely aware of the curious voices on the street below.

He grabs my hands and squeezes them as he sits up and looks around. Before I know it, he releases me and turns into that familiar stream of sparkles, going from chimney to chimney despite the onlookers below.

He comes back a few minutes later with a bag that is significantly lighter than before. He just smiles, unties the reins, and snaps them.

We are off once again. The rest of the Eastern Hemisphere goes without another attack, and it isn't until we're over the Atlantic Ocean that I feel the knot between my shoulders unwind for a moment.

"I've never been able to heal wounds with Christmas magic," Santa says softly. "Maybe produce a bandage out of thin air, but you mended my skin like their claws never tore through it." His voice is low, as if speaking of the deed will undo what I did.

"I healed Blitzen too." I wave toward the last reindeer in the pack.

"I don't know if you noticed, but we're back on track, as well. Whatever you did electrified all of us." Dad slides his gaze to me, and the reindeer nod in unison.

I laugh and wave his words away. "Without—"

"Don't brush this away like it isn't something incredibly special," he says in that stern tone of his.

It's almost a reprimand, but I'm old enough to merely roll my eyes.

"I kill monsters for a living, Dad." I can't think of anything else to say, and frankly, it's slightly embarrassing to be called out for a gift you have only one day a year. "Besides, this"— I raise my hands—"is Christmas magic. I only have it while we're delivering gifts to the world's children." I shrug and bring my hands back to my lap, where they wrestle together as I fidget under his stark gaze.

"How did you do it?"

I press my lips together as I consider the question. When I stroked Blitzen and wiped his wounds away, I simply believed I was able to heal him with that touch because of the Christmas magic swelling inside me. Same with my father.

As lights of another city dance in the distance, I glance at him. "You taught me Christmas is a time of miracles, and I believed."

SILENT NIGHT CHAPTER 6

I ALWASYS FIND THE South American landscape to be awe-inspiring. The thick jungle alongside the mountains rivals the Alaskan countryside and even that of the North Pole, in my opinion.

And the islands in the Caribbean all decked out in Christmas cheer are charming without seeming cheesy. My grin seems to be a constant staple as we island-hop our way to the southern tip of Florida in the United States.

This year, we decide to do a zigzag from south to north and east to west, so we can take advantage of the time differences in order to get home before my mother's meal is ruined. Since I healed my father, he seems to be fueled by something, making him unnaturally faster, and we have more than made up for the initial slowness as well as the time we lost during the monster attacks in the Eastern Hemisphere.

Thankfully, outside of the initial attack in New Zealand, the Southern Hemisphere has been calm. But that changes when we reach the interior of the Northeast near the Canadian border. It's as if an entire herd of perytons were waiting for us to arrive.

It's hard to miss the horde as it approaches due south to our northern heading. My heart rate picks up and I stand, hopping onto the front edge of the sleigh as I unsheathe Joy. She tingles in my hands as "I'll Be Home for Christmas" slashes across the night sky, with both my father's and my voices joining in. When the reindeer start to sing, the magic of Christmas encompasses the reindeer in a cocoon of comfort.

But it leaves Santa and me vulnerable.

"Move forward a little," I say between choruses, jumping onto the seat behind him. He leans into me, pinning me to the back of the sleigh so I can't tumble out, and gives me a grim nod.

His suit is still in tatters from the gargoyle attack, and if the perytons get within range to shish kabab him on their antlers, that could prove to be more devastating than the last attack. The gargoyles had not gotten to his heart, but a well-placed antler could spear right through it.

"What's the plan?" Dad asks, still steering straight for the pack.

"Use the magic surrounding the reindeer. It acts like my sword and if any get through, well, Joy will do the job."

"So, instead of evasive action, we play a little chicken." My father grins and that light that always seems to be in his eyes brightens.

Santa is enjoying the idea of battle, like he used to enjoy our sparring sessions while he taught me the different forms of martial arts. I didn't think I'd live to see the day where we would be in a fight together, but the shine in his smile tells me his adrenaline is running just as high as mine, even without a weapon.

"I'll be Home for Christmas" transitions to "We Need a Little Christmas," and our voices seem to echo off the land.

Dad steers the sleigh straight for the perytons and after the leading ones hit the magical barrier around the reindeer, and turn into a glitter storm, the rest of the perytons scatter like seagulls when a child runs right for them on a beach.

Santa pursues a group that veer to the right as I spin Joy over my head, protecting us from above. But that leaves us vulnerable on both sides. I keep sweeping my gaze back and forth to ensure that an attack is not coming in either direction.

The reindeer sing louder as they dash from peryton to the next peryton, laughing with joy as the beasts explode into glitter when the barrier hits them. I guess it's better than sending torrents of blood over us.

Joy transitions to "Feliz Navidad," and the upbeat tempo seems to give us all an extra boost. I'm swinging away around us, chopping down those that try to attack from the sides, when a sudden sting throws me forward. I nearly lose Joy as I sail over the front of the sleigh.

It takes me a moment to realize my left shoulder is impaled on one of the monster's antlers. Pain flares, and I cry out as it lifts me higher, away from the sleigh. Santa looks up at me with wide eyes. He doesn't see the two perytons aiming at his blind side.

"Bank right!" I call out, and the reindeer do as I say, still singing the song that Joy leads. I cannot see the sleigh below to make sure they turned in time to save my father from the same fate.

I snarl as the peryton takes me higher and farther from Santa. I swing Joy behind me and am rewarded with a puff of glitter. Then gravity takes hold and I'm in a free fall, without the sleigh or reindeer below to catch me. Another peryton charges for me in the sky. The blaze in its eyes makes me swallow hard. His antlers are longer than my sword.

The singing becomes louder, surrounding me like a warm blanket. I don't dare deviate my attention away from the murderous beast charging at me, or look at the drop below that would certainly steal my life away. Magic strokes my skin, reaching for me, pulling me back to safety.

Before the beast reaches me, Dasher comes up beneath me, and I land on his back with a thump that sends air rushing from my lips. And yet again, I almost lose my grip on Joy.

My shoulder screams upon impact, but no sound escapes from my mouth as I try to make my lungs pull air in instead of feeling this vortex sucking my last breath from me. The barrier in front of Dasher and Dancer rams into the peryton who thought he'd target me, turning him into a plume of colorful glitter.

I swing my gaze around, looking for the rest of the monsters, but the sky is empty. It seems we annihilated all of them, or the survivors decided they liked living more than whatever deal they had made to take down Santa.

I wish I had a chance to pry a name from their dirty mouths.

I wish I had a target for this unhealthy anger rising inside me.

"That was the last one," Santa calls to me.

I turn and nod, sliding Joy back into her sheath. Before I climb off Dasher, I stroke his head and neck and give him a hug.

"Thanks for saving my ass," I whisper.

"Thanks for saving all our asses," he says back, glancing over his shoulder. "Lord knows some of us are not worthy." His cheeks turn red, and he faces forward.

"You and Dancer are worthy."

He huffs at me. "We didn't realize that eggnog was spiked," he replies softly. "It was just left outside by the back door for anyone to get into, and it smelled so good."

I blink and look at the two reindeer. "You didn't sneak a drink through the kitchen window to get it?"

They shake their heads. "That is *not* allowed." Only one reindeer would break the rules without so much as a reprimand, and he had been more blitzed than these two. "Besides, Rudolph found it first, and Dancer and I just wanted a taste," Dasher adds. "Tell Santa we're very sorry."

"I will." I pat his neck. "But I think you just made up for it." I climb off him onto the pole connecting all the reindeer to the sleigh. "You didn't happen to see who put the bowl out, did you?"

"No, we didn't," both Dasher and Dancer say at the same time.

Disappointment laces my mouth, overriding the dull throbbing in my shoulder. I head forward, with my gaze dancing around the sky, looking for the next attack. When I glance at my father, his brow furrows with worry.

I step over the front of the sleigh and collapse onto the seat next to him.

"You're injured." His voice holds pain and anguish.

I glance down at my shoulder and try not to wince as I take stock of my torn jacket and the equally damaged skin beneath. At least the monster was kind enough not to hit any bone. It's a clean shot right through me. "It'll heal."

My father hands me the reins, then takes hold of both sides of my body. He closes his eyes, and a deep crease appears as he brings his eyebrows together in concentration. His cheeks turn red, and finally, opens his eyes once more.

"What are you trying to do?" I cock an eyebrow at him.

He drops his hands and stares at his bloody palms as though they failed him in some manner. With a sigh and a wiggle of his fingers, he has two of those bandages with the self-stick edges. "Lean forward," he says, proceeding to patch up the entry and exit wounds.

SILENT NIGHT CHAPTER 7

WE CONTINUE DELIVERING GIFTS as if it were just another normal Christmas Eve. But tonight has been anything but normal, as evidenced by my father's nearly shredded and blood-stained suit and my torn jacket. Black leather doesn't show blood the way his white fur does, and I stare at the stains as he settles into the seat next to me. My wound itches and I shift in the seat, stanching the overriding need to scratch at it.

"Who would want you dead?" I meet his gaze with my own.

He purses his lips, as if there is a long list to consider, and as he looks out at the reindeer, he sighs and snaps the reins.

It's all a bit unnerving.

"Is there someone?" I press, because his reaction is not what I had expected.

"There could be a few. I got a little ornery with some of the elves the other day when they tried to bring up making my toy factory a union shop."

I snort a laugh. "Union? Why do they want a union?"

"Fair wages, reasonable hours, ability to move up in the ranks. That's what they spouted." He sighs and wipes his face. "All the normal things a union shop wants to control. And I got the explicit feeling that the last demand was the most important. Even though there is no true upward movement among elves. Sure, they can go from toy making to management, but that's as high as they can go. Unless they're vying for my job, but that isn't possible."

I chuckle and shake my head. "Union shop at the North Pole. What a farce."

He glances over at me with a nod. "That was my reaction. And apparently it angered some of the boys."

I am compelled to point out the obvious. "Anger and premeditated murder are two different beasts."

Santa shrugs. "True. But I'd know who, along with the very reason why, if we were being attacked by an actual person. The naughty list would spell it out for me like a neon beacon." He directs the reindeer toward a nearby neighborhood. "Elves and monsters are not on any of my lists." He glances at me again. "And the only beings with enough magic at their disposal to control the monsters reside in or around the North Pole."

"We need to figure out who's behind all this." I scan the horizon. My gaze sweeps back and forth restlessly and my shoulder throbs in time with my heart. "What about the Winter Warlock?"

Santa rolls his eyes. "It isn't a witch or a warlock. They are on my list. I would know if it was one of their kind."

"Yes, but the Winter Warlock *was* evil in the past."

My father sighs. "He was never evil. He was just lonely, and while he did scare people, he never harmed a soul. Besides, he's not the type who would put out a filthy contract on my life. If he wanted me dead, he wouldn't leave it to anyone else to do the deed. He would do it himself."

My father is entirely too trusting. I pinch the bridge of my nose, thinking I don't discount the Winter Warlock as a suspect. He has enough magic to control monsters, after all. "Who were the elves that asked about turning our toy shop into a union shop?"

"Sunny and Vale."

The oldest damn elf in the entire North Pole, along with one of the dumbest. I wipe my face as we land on another roof. Then I give my father a strained smile, and he swirls into action, delivering gifts to the houses around us while I mull over the two names.

Sunny isn't just the oldest, either. He's in charge of the reindeer on Christmas Eve, as well as the toy factory.

"Did anyone see who left the eggnog out?" I ask, and the exasperation of our situation bleeds through into my voice.

Cupid cocks his head as he turns toward me. "I didn't see who left it out, but I'm pretty sure it was Elise who took the empty eggnog container inside. She didn't look happy about it, either. I caught some of her mutterings about who under the heavens left the eggnog pot outside, of all places.”

“Elise?” Elise is Sunny’s wife, and she’s in charge of the kitchen on most days. She makes a scrumptious Christmas cookie, too. I bite my lower lip as Cupid nods at me. She is not naturally chipper like most elves. She practically glowers at me whenever I come home, whereas the others smile and flit around me, asking a thousand and one questions.

The lights dance back into the seat next to me before they form back into my father.

I tell him, “Cupid says Elise brought the bowl in from outside, but she seemed agitated with it not being in the right place.” I tilt my head. “Do you think Sunny could be angry enough that he would manipulate the monsters to try to kill you?”

Santa levels his gaze at me, shaking his head. “You might want to stick with monster slaying. Your sleuth skills seem to be lacking.” He snaps the reins, and we are off to the next neighborhood.

“Dad, I thought you said I could do anything if I put my mind to it.” I cross my arms and slouch in my spot next to him on the seat. But that doesn’t stop me from keeping a sharp eye on all that surrounds us. My nerves tingle, telling me the danger is far from over.

My sideways glance at my father reveals that tic in his jaw that he usually has when he's clenching it. The jolly Santa I'm used to is nowhere to be found. He is just as on edge as I feel.

"You can, but I doubt we'll be able to solve this mystery tonight. Not when I have a job to do and a time limit in which it must be done." He sends his own strained smile my way. "In other words, I can't focus on this until we have a reprieve over the Pacific."

We land effortlessly. And then he is gone in a sprinkle of light.

I run my hand over my face. "God above, give me the strength to keep him safe tonight." I glance at the heavens. My injury saps a little more of my power as the evening wears on.

If we have to battle more gargoyles and perytons, I'm not sure I have the strength to keep them at bay. Not with a bum shoulder that stings every time I shift my weight. Even with Joy and Christmas magic at our disposal. I lean my head back against the hilt of my sword, and it vibrates as if it's trying to tell me all will be well.

I smile and sigh. My sword is even more optimistic than I am. I start to sing the song that inspired me to name my sword.

"Joy to the world, the Lord is come. Let Earth receive her King." The reindeer join in, and the song drifts softly over me. Magic tingles in my fingertips and down my spine as it takes hold of me.

The Christmas spirit is still alive and vibrant, and it fills me with the same emotion as my sword's namesake. I smile at the stars above, and all my doubt is erased away.

I truly believe in the magic of this season.

SILENT NIGHT CHAPTER 8

IT ISN'T UNTIL WE are north of Mt. Rainier and heading toward Seattle that another disturbance appears in the distance. On the West Coast, there's more cloud cover than the rest of the country, and it is hard to discern clouds from real threats.

My muscles tense. The tic in my father's tight jaw is back and it seems he stiffens as well. I rise to my feet, ignoring the protest of all my muscles, especially my shoulder, which sings a very loud and obnoxious tune of pain.

I pull Joy from her sleeve.

"Holly Jolly Christmas" rings out around us. I usually join in on this song, but I'm feeling sluggish and the best I can do is whisper the words. However, both the reindeer and my father seem to be all in with the song, sparking magic in the night.

I squint as the clouds move in a strange manner. We are vulnerable here and don't have enough power to wrap the sleigh and the reindeer in our protective buffer. I glance up at the thick cloud cover once more. If we were above this cover, it would be easier to defend the sleigh.

"Go up. Above the clouds."

My father looks at me and then at the approaching mass, then pulls the reins back. The reindeer shoot almost vertically up, and I slam into the seat with the force. Thankfully, I don't tumble right over the back or lose hold of Joy.

As soon as we clear the cloud cover, the moon shines over the layer, making it look silver against the black sky. We continue singing, and the magical barrier stretches out below us.

Something bumps into the sleigh, and a familiar burst happens. In front of us, nearly a half dozen monsters hit the barrier, and they burst into Christmas glitter. I am unsure what these are until one plunges through the clouds to the side of the sleigh.

"Duck!" I yell at Santa before swinging in the direction of the gargoyle that reaches for him. Joy slices through meat and bone, and then the ugly thing turns to glitter.

"Behind you!" he cries to me.

Instead of stopping my swing, I spin, bringing Joy with me.

The gargoyle is closer than the other one. Close enough for its claws to reach me. But I throw my injured arm up in a block, wincing at the drag of claws down my forearm just before the beast meets Joy and bursts into glitter.

I sit down hard, breathing out in heaving pulls as my gaze travels around us to be sure we aren't still under attack. When my gut tells me we're safe, I slide Joy back into her holder and give my father a nod.

He turns the sleigh, plummeting through the clouds to the next roof. Instead of immediately getting out, he conjures another bandage and wraps my arm in silence. His gaze locks on my face, and then he sits back in the seat once he's done.

"This is what you do every day?"

I chuckle and shrug. "I usually don't get impaled on an antler, but yes. This is my job." He's seen me dispatch a monster or two before when we've run across them, but it was rare, and it usually happened in remote areas like the Himalayas or the Andes. "Go. Time is ticking," I say with a nod toward the chimney.

In a blink, he turns into that magic stream of light.

I close my eyes for a moment and then reach down under the dash of the sleigh, where I slipped a bottle of water before we set out. Thankfully, it hadn't been dislodged and lost in all our evasive maneuvers throughout the night. I crack it open and take a sip. The cool liquid slides down my throat like it was heaven-sent. I cap it and stow it back where I found it, relishing the silence of the early hour.

As we go north, we might hit some snow. I smile at the prospect.

A scream shatters the night, and I'm instantly on my feet, scanning the street below. My father stumbles out the front door of the last house he had magically descended into the chimney to deliver his gifts. He makes it as far as the road and then falls to his knees.

"Go!" I shout and the reindeer take off, landing right beside him on the wet asphalt.

I'm out, with Joy in my hands. I don't even look up at my surroundings as both Joy and the reindeer sing in the night. My father's neck is slashed, and he glances at me as if all is lost.

I lay Joy across his chest and put my hands on both sides of his throat. Joy switches to "Silent Night," my particular power song, while I sing along and push all my healing magic into my father. His neck mends as Christmas magic swirls around us. My father's eyes blink closed, and I will him to live, even if it means taking every last ounce of my life force.

Santa is still pale, but his neck shows no sign of the gaping wound it had when he fell in the street. His chest rises and falls in even beats. I look up past the trail of blood, and a small child stands at the door of the house with her hand over her mouth.

I climb to my feet, leaving Joy on my father to protect him while I pull daggers from my sheath. Whoever or whatever hurt my father is in this house, and they need to pay.

"Is Santa...dead?" the child asks, her eyes wide and terrified.

I glance at the open space behind her and shake my head. "No, he's resting." Then I crouch down to her level. If this child hadn't screamed, we would have never known my father was in danger. "Did you see who hurt him?"

Her eyes are almost too wide, and her little form starts shaking as if it's freezing out. She nods. "A m-monster," she whispers as her teeth start chattering.

"Is it still in there?"

Her eyes rise to look at something over my shoulder. That's when my brain registers Joy's music growing close. I turn and see Santa standing behind me, with Joy in his hand.

"Stay with her. I have a monster to slay."

"Are you sure you don't want me to take care of this?" I should be the one to kill the monster, but the anger in my father's eyes gives me pause. When he shakes his head, I add, "See if you can find out who is orchestrating this before you deal the final blow."

He nods, stepping around me and the wide-eyed child shivering in the night.

I wonder where her parents are. "Thank you for alerting us," I say, and her gaze moves from my father to me and my bloody hands.

Her chin quivers. "I wasn't supposed to get out of bed until the morning," she whispers.

I want to run my hand through her hair and give her a hug, but I doubt her parents would appreciate waking up to her having dried blood all over her. Although, from the look of the entryway, there is a trail of blood from their living room to the front stoop. The deep timbre of voices rolls out through the hall, and I strain to try to hear the words. But then glitter bursts into the hallway, landing in the red liquid smearing the floors.

Santa walks out with Joy leaning on his shoulder, still singing her Christmas tunes. He swirls his finger, and a small tornado follows him, cleaning up the mess the monster left behind.

I stand as the glitter and blood join in the cleaning twister, following him out to the porch. He hands me the sword with his lips pressed tightly together. Then he nods and turns his attention to the child.

"Dear Samantha, I am sorry you had to see that unfortunate incident. Your house is monster-free now." He smiles at her and pats her head. "Thank you for the cookies and milk. Now you need to go back to your room and back to sleep so all this seems like a bad dream when you wake up." He turns her and scooches her inside, watching as she heads upstairs. Once she is out of sight, he closes the door and marches past me to the sled. The cleaning swirl follows him, erasing the evidence of his near death.

I slide Joy into my sheath, silencing her as I follow and climb into the far side of the sleigh.

SILENT NIGHT CHAPTER 9

MY FATHER DOESN'T SPEAK but he does accept one of my daggers and slides it into his belt before he finishes delivering gifts throughout the rest of North America. Even the light snow doesn't lift his sour mood.

Thankfully, there are no more attacks on the mainland of North America as we finish up our deliveries through Alaska and head south over the Pacific for Hawaii, Midway, and lastly the Baker Islands.

"Do you know who ordered the hit?" I ask, because that is what this is: a hit on his life. I'm not sure whether the attack on me outside the portal was part of this ungodly plan to kill Santa, but it certainly would have made the monsters successful without me there to defend him.

He gives me a curt nod. "The gargoyle overestimated himself." He huffs a laugh. "Or sorely underestimated you. He said he already sent the success message before that child started screaming. They think the monsters killed me." His gaze slashes to mine, and a smile like nothing I've ever seen appears on his face. It's cold and dangerous. "We have the element of surprise."

A shiver slides down my side as my brain catches up. There is one person he's forgetting. "What about Mom?" My heart picks up at the sudden shift in him and the way he snaps the reins, demanding more speed.

"I have to hope they will not harm her," he says. But now that I've asked the question, worry overshadows the anger on his brow. He takes a breath. "We'll have the reindeer drop us off outside before they land in the courtyard."

"And then what? What's your plan?" I lean toward him, and the reindeers' ears shift to catch the conversation.

He looks at the creatures in front of us. "They will only fly for the true Santa, not the traitor who wishes to take over." His lips cock into an evil grin. "That's when we come in from the house, and you can spread Joy around at will."

I blink at him. "How many?"

"Only one gave the orders, according to the gargoyle. Dark magic animated them and controlled them, and that's how they communicated the failures along the way. It's how they lined up the next attack when one failed. Without the black magic animating them, they would have never dreamed of attacking us. And the peryton? Who the hell knows how they got where they were, but I'm willing to bet black magic played a hand in gathering them, too. If I had been certain the gargoyle wouldn't report back to them, I would have let it live. But I've never trusted the reach of black magic. And with your mom at their mercy, we need that element of surprise." He stares out at the darkness surrounding us and sighs. "I'm not entirely convinced that Sunny is aware of this diabolical plan, either."

My brow furrows as my brain catches up. Sunny and Vale came to him about the union, but it couldn't be Vale. Vale couldn't conjure a bow to finish off the wrappings on a Christmas gift, never mind control an entire population of monsters.

My eyes widen as the only other logical elf rises to the surface. "Elise gave the orders?"

He nods. "I wouldn't eat whatever she has prepared tonight, either. I wouldn't put it past her to plan on poisoning every last one of us to get what she wants. There are going to be a lot of hungry and very angry elves tonight."

As soon as we're finished in the Pacific, Santa races to the portal and we barrel through it, stopping outside the towering drifts. We hop off and watch as the unmanned sleigh swirls up and around the peaks to the North Pole and Santa's courtyard.

Usually, Christmas music echoes off the surrounding mountains upon Dad's arrival, but only quiet lingers. In the distance, I swear I hear sobbing.

I glance over at my father.

"I hope your mother forgives me for this little ruse," he says softly before starting for the snowdrift maze and our home with me at his side.

SILENT NIGHT CHAPTER 10

WE STEP IN THE house together. Me in my ruined leather jacket and Santa in his blood-soaked, shredded suit with the blade still stuck in his belt. He didn't need it for the last leg, but he kept it close just in case. He looks just as badass as I feel as we head toward the side entrance to the courtyard.

We stick to the shadows, and all I can hear is a high-pitched female voice trying to calm the crowd of devastated elves. Mom is on her knees, sobbing by the side of the blood-splashed sleigh for the loss of her husband and daughter.

It tears my insides apart more acutely than any of those monsters could. My father's eyes carry the same hurt. Fury rides through every muscle of mine, making my shoulder pound with my increased heartbeat.

The reindeer shift from foot to foot, looking in our direction before trading glances but they keep quiet, just as they should. Even their eyes carry the hard edge of anger.

Sunny comes out of the back door from the main house into the courtyard, wearing the full Santa garb with his arms extended, as if he owns the place. Yet the elf is only a fraction of my father's height and does not instill the same Christmas spirit as the true Santa, despite his overexuberant "Ho-ho-ho."

He slides into the sleigh as though he's going to drive it back to the garage, but the reindeer don't budge when he prompts them by snapping the reins. His expression falls as he looks at the reins, as if the problem lies in the leather ties in his hands.

The reindeer know he isn't in charge of them. They heard my father talking about Sunny's plans on the sleigh. This elf and his wife were responsible for the near death of their beloved Santa. They send a sneer in Sunny's direction, looking at him with all the animosity I feel.

"Jess will be the new cook," Elise announces, waving to my mother as if it is an honor in itself. "And because Sunny is the oldest elf, older than Santa himself, he and I will take up residence in the main house." She smiles sweetly, as if she hadn't planned all this with her husband. "We will make this place run like a well-oiled clock!"

As if it didn't already run smoothly. My fists clench, as do my teeth. Rage coils in my belly, turning into a force of its own.

Sunny snaps the reins again, but the sleigh does not budge. "Move, you filthy bastards!"

I trade a glance with my father. Storm clouds gather in his eyes, and thunder rumbles overhead despite the clear skies.

Sunny glances up, and concern paints his brow. He snaps the reins again, to no avail. The reindeer refuse to budge for the fake Santa.

Dad nods, and we step out of the shadows. I draw Joy from my scabbard, and the chilling tune of "The Little Drummer Boy" slices through the silence.

Gasps fill the area, and the crowd parts.

All I see is red when I stare at the two complicit traitors. Vengeance roars up in my blood, and all I want to do is strike them down. No explanation will appease this immense need for justice.

They are monsters, and it is my job to extinguish the unholy beasts.

Elise's eyes widen and then narrow as she realizes her plans of dominating the North Pole have been thwarted. Her face scrunches in frustrated anger.

"Chris!" my mother's voice rings out with relief, and then she is on her feet.

As she runs by Elise, the little witch shoots out her leg, sending my mother to the ground. Then she grabs my mother by the hair and yanks her back onto her knees. From out of nowhere, a knife appears at Mom's throat. "Strike your father down, and I will let your mother live."

Everyone freezes. The somber song plays on, and I glance at Santa. His eyes fill with pain, and he gives me a nod. He wishes to forfeit his life for hers. That is how strong his love is for my mother.

I shake my head. I cannot strike my father down, even if that is his solution to keeping the love of his life alive.

I don't know what Elise expected, but from the snarl she emits, this was not it. "You all think you're better than us. That you are above the elves. You can't even agree to a union to protect us from dangerous work conditions." Elise waves the knife toward us and then places it back against my mother's throat. "And then you bitch and whine about the food placed on your tables, as if it isn't good enough or varied enough or sweet enough. I want more than just an elf's existence. I want to be respected and revered!"

She's screaming now, and all I can do is stare at the knife scraping up and down Mom's throat, leaving a red mark like a rug burn on her skin. The knife hasn't broken the skin yet, but my gut tells me it's only a matter of time.

"I want to be waited on and pampered. I want what you have. Strike him down so I can have the power I crave!" The pitch of her screech echoes off the buildings surrounding us.

I look at my father and know I shouldn't say it, but it rolls out of my mouth before I can stop it. "She's an angry elf."

Santa smirks and nods despite the dangerous tension filling the air.

"That's it." Elise stomps her foot like an irate two-year-old. "You have to the count of three to do as I say, or I will kill your mother."

Black smoke cascades out of Elise like a vile disease. Even Sunny's eyes bug out at her. "One!"

She must be stopped.

Electricity crackles through the air as Joy's volume rises. The reindeer join in singing "The Little Drummer Boy," and so do the elves around us.

They know. They understand the magnitude of what Christmas magic can do.

It is so much more powerful than black magic.

"Two!" Elise screeches.

"Ferret out the monsters," I whisper, planting Joy into the ground between my feet. Magic blasts through the snow like an ever-expanding wave made of blinding white light. Then it narrows into two straight beams.

One goes straight through my mother, widening her eyes and blowing her hair back before it barrels into Elise, exploding the elf into a rocket of fireworks and glitter. The second does the same to Sunny. If there had been any others in on this vile attempt on my father's life, my magic would have taken them out just as efficiently.

But there were only two traitors in our midst.

The knife Elise held drops harmlessly in front of Mom, sticking blade-down in the snow.

Gasps ring out over the courtyard, nearly drowning out the last note of the song resounding from Joy. I pull her from the ground and slip her back into her sheath. Silence blankets us.

And then my mother is on her feet, sprinting into Santa's arms. After a long, tight squeeze, she pulls away and begins frantically looking for the injuries that caused his coat to be soiled with blood. But she cannot find the source.

My father grabs her hands and tilts her chin up so she meets his gaze. "You will not find a scratch on me." He smiles down at her as his eyes sparkle with adoration.

"But how?" My mother waves at the obvious destruction of his suit.

He nods toward me. "Chrissy used Christmas magic to heal me."

"Me, too!" shouts Blitzen.

She turns to me, blinking madly as if her brain cannot comprehend the power of

Christmas, even after the latest display. She rakes her eyes over my disheveled and torn coat, along with the patches covering my wounds on my arms and shoulder, but she does not leave my father's embrace.

I, unlike my father, am not healed. I offer her a smile and a shrug. "I might be in need of a doctor." I glance at the patches on my arm. Deep brownish-red spots show through the bandages.

"We will patch you up and then sit down for the feast," my mother says.

Her declaration seems to knock the elves back from the shock of seeing two of their own turn into glitter. They rush toward us as if they are welcoming us back from the dead.

"Um. About that. We might not want to trust the food that Elise made. It's probably tainted in some way," Santa says.

It only takes a moment before the entirety of the group groans at the prospect of not having a Christmas feast.

I glance around, and my gaze lands on the Winter Warlock. Even he looks troubled. He meets my gaze and steps forward.

"Perhaps I can help detect what may be tainted," he says almost sheepishly.

I smile at him, admonishing myself for even thinking this gentle giant of a man could ever have an evil bone in his body. "That would be nice."

"And then I can see what I can do for your wounds." He nods toward my soiled bandages.

I don't agree to that quite yet. I am more worried about poisoned food than a few drops of lost blood, so we lead him into the grand banquet room, where our tree reaches to the rafters and sparkles with lights and golden garland.

The banquet table stretches the entire length of the room with enough seating for the entire village. It's decorated in shades of red and green with gold and silver accents. A braid of evergreen stretches down the middle, illuminated by Christmas lights. Just like Santa's suit, it is a tradition and beautifully executed.

I suck in a breath and look at the serving tables. Dozens of dishes are laid out across them, with enough to feed us all for the next twelve days.

The Winter Warlock closes his eyes, and his hands move in smooth figure eights, creating a rainbow of sparkling magic. When he stretches his arms out, the colorful magic races to the buffet, leaping from dish to dish, swirling around them before jumping to the next.

Some dishes brighten and others turn to a pale gray mush as the magic touches them.

When his magic has touched all the dishes, it returns to him, filling his form with the rainbow spectrum before fading.

All the dishes Dad usually loads his plate with are all gray mush. Poisoned to make sure if we made it back alive, my father wouldn't survive the Christmas feast.

"Damn that elf," Santa says under his breath as he scans the table.

A quarter of the dishes need to go. With another push of the warlock's magic, the gray mush turns to smoke, disappearing from the tables altogether. The warlock's lips pull down into a deep frown as he shakes his head.

"They apparently did not care about collateral damage in their quest for power," he snaps, meeting my gaze. "Let's see what I can do for you."

"They didn't care about anyone but themselves." I look over what food remains, and my stomach roars to life. "My wounds can wait. My stomach can't."

We dig into what remains of the feast, loading our plates and taking a seat at the banquet table, trying to rekindle the true Christmas spirit.

And after we thank the Lord for the food before us as well as our safe return, the Winter Warlock asks, "Now tell us what in the Hades happened to you tonight."

Santa glances over at Mom and gently kisses her cheek before sending me a wink.

"It started off as a clear and silent night…" My father launches into the story of our harrowing Christmas Eve, with all the magic of a master storyteller.

The End

Thank you for reading SILENT NIGHT!

Continue on the next page with CHRISTMAS WISH.

SILENT NIGHT TRILOGY

BOOK THREE

CHRISTMAS WISH

Tanya Snow has been searching for the right elf for…well, forever. But he's not in the North Pole. Believe me, she's dated all the eligible elves there are, even those in farther settlements, but none of them has caused her snow-laden heart to thaw.

She's the flurry queen, and without a king to settle by her side, I'm afraid the winters will get more brutal and unpredictable.

Even Santa has noticed, and when he calls on me to talk my best friend off the ledge, I can't say no. Especially not to my father. But playing matchmaker in the big city isn't one of my main skills, I'm not sure I can find Mr. Right, or even Mr. Right Now, to sway her frosty disposition.

Besides, New York City isn't ready for a force like Tanya Snow.

CHRISTMAS WISH
CHAPTER 1

MONSTER HUNTING HAD BEEN sporadic since Christmas. It was like the beasts went into hiding after that nearly disastrous night protecting my father on his annual sleigh run.

Although, later today, I did have a client meeting scheduled. The first one in a couple of months, and I was getting desperate for the money. My reserves had bled down with the lack of activity, but I needed a little beach time relaxation before I jumped headfirst into another dangerous job.

I settled into a prime spot on the sand and opened my book with every intention of enjoying a lovely morning lounging in the sun, but my Kringle intuition bloomed in my chest. I shifted my position, trying to ease the sensation that all this calm was about to explode into a million deadly shards.

The shrill ring of "Santa Claus is Coming to Town" shattered the quiet, and my mood jumped right into sheer panic. The few folks on the beach at this early hour sent raised eyebrows in my direction at my choice of ringtone.

I snatched the phone before the stanza had even come to an end. My heart pumped hard in my chest. My father never called during the summer months. I swiped the screen to accept the call and put the phone to my ear.

"Dad?" I could't help the trepidation in my voice.

A sigh followed. "Chrissy." His baritone voice held a tremor.

I gulped. "Is Mom okay?"

"Yes." His tone was clipped as if he had been clenching his jaw. "I need your help."

I hopped to my feet and collected my stuff off the sand, and then headed toward the parking lot and my motorcycle waiting to take me back to the city. "I'm on my way."

"I'll see you when you get here. Oh, and Chrissy?"

"Yeah?"

"Wear warm shoes." He disconnected the call.

I stared at the phone. While it was the North Pole, it was also the middle of July. And July was the only time the North Pole thawed, revealing the green of rolling hills and unfrosted pines. The elves swam in the crystal-clear pond in the center of town, just like so many others looking for the relief from the summer heat.

The minute I got back to my little apartment, I slipped into jeans and debated on my flip-flops. I pulled on one of my black T-shirts and then decided that because I needed to hustle, sneakers were probably more ideal. I grabbed my light fall jacket off the coat-tree near the door and balled it up into my bag, before locking up behind me.

The summer heat slammed into me when I stepped out onto the street. I was glad my hair was up in a single ponytail, but the humidity still made my scalp sweat. By the time I reached the portal in Soho, all I wanted to do was peel out of these clothes.

Anxious to get out of this oppressive heat, I stepped up to the portal and swiped my thumb over the sensor that recognized me and let the ether suck me through to the other side. The sensation was jarring, especially since I left New York to the tune of ninety-some-degree weather and stepped out into a snowstorm.

"What the..."

I dug in my bag for the coat so my clothing wouldn't be soaked through by the time I got to my childhood home. My sneakered feet sank into the snowbank. I slid my coat on and shouldered the bag, trudging through the snow as my toes squished inside my now soggy shoes.

At least I had opted for sneakers. I had originally had my flip-flops on and that would have left me open to a toe or two getting frostbit on my trek to the house.

My dad hadn't been kidding. I circled around the snow drifts buffering the North Pole from the rest of the landscape like I had done on so many Christmas Eve mornings coming home to do my annual job of protecting Santa.

When the town came into view my stomach dropped. It looked barren without the holiday decorations. I guess I had never noticed that while I lived here as a child, but since I moved to New York City, I hadn't seen the town bathed in snow without holiday adornments. I had come in at the height of the July heat before, and the rolling green hills framed our little town with only the higher elevations capped in white.

By the time I stepped into the house, my jeans were frozen from the snow, and my feet were sopping wet and uncomfortable. I pushed the door against the raging wind until it closed. I didn't think we'd had this kind of storm since before I was born. I certainly didn't remember the wind being so vicious.

My father stepped into the hallway. Just one look at my dad told me that his mood was dark.

"What's with the snowstorm?" I waved at the door behind me before I squatted down to untie my frozen laces.

"Tanya and the elf she had been dating broke up."

I sucked air through my teeth. Tanya Snow, my oldest and dearest friend, was certainly a wild card. Even when we were little, playing with our dolls, she had been enamored by the idea of love. As she got older, she had breezed through the entire line up of eligible elves while looking for a match, but it seemed to evade her like a criminal running from the police. At least up here at the North Pole.

"Wasn't that the last eligible elf?"

His lips pursed, and he gave me a curt nod. "Thus, the weather."

"He broke it off?"

A gale of wind howled down the chimney in response.

"What do you think?"

It wasn't like my father to be so snarky. That was my job, not his, but he must've been at his wits end.

Tanya's obviously overly emotional state had triggered the storm. It used to happen when we were little when she got upset, and as she aged, the storms got more severe when her heart broke.

Plus, this was summertime. It was the time for my father to relax and soak in some rays. That wasn't happening at the moment, and he seemed to be starved of the vitamin D he desperately needed to keep his jolliness intact.

I wasn't sure why he summoned me to the North Pole, except to rant about Snow. He could have done that over the phone.

"So, what do you need me to do?"

"I need you to talk to her, maybe take her out for a drink or something. She needs a diversion, and we need summer to return. Otherwise, we'll be buried in snow come winter."

I snorted a laugh at him. "I have a meeting for a job this afternoon."

I didn't want to tell him I needed this job to pay the rent.

"If she continues to wallow in self-pity, I may just strangle her."

I blinked, stood, and slipped off my wet shoes, surprised at the venom in his voice. "And you think I won't?"

After all, Santa Claus was probably the most patient man on earth. If she got barbs under his skin, what hope did I have.

"You're her friend. Talk to her before she completely ruins Christmas this year. The snow is disrupting the supply chain. Toys will not be completed in time for Christmas if this continues." His glare hit me along with his words.

"Is anything open here?" I waved at the storm beyond the door.

He glanced out the window and then back at me with a shrug. "Bring a bottle of wine over to her house. Just get her to calm the hell down. Give her a diversion she needs to get out of her funk and give the rest of us a break."

I wiped my face. "What about my job?"

His eyes hardened. "Look. I haven't asked a lot of you since you decided to leave us. I've let you have your own life, make your own choices, even though it sometimes pains your mother and me, but I'm asking for your help now."

His hands found his hips as he stared me down.

Well, crap on a cracker. I couldn't say no to my dad. And he was right. He had given me all the latitude to live my own life, and he had supported me when the elves gave me the job to keep him safe on his Christmas Eve trek.

"Fine." I threw my hands up in the air and headed toward the stairs.

"Where are you going?"

I stopped on the third stair and waved at my wet pants and socks that were leaving small water prints where I had walked. "I need dry clothing more appropriate for a snowstorm."

His gaze dropped to the darkness of my pants from the knees down and then gave me a nod.

I headed to my childhood room and the clothes I had left there on purpose. I peeled off my wet jeans and traded them for fur-lined leggings, which I would totally regret once I stepped through the portal, but they would keep me dry while cutting through the snowy walk to the house of one of my oldest childhood friends.

CHRISTMAS WISH
CHAPTER 2

I DUSTED OFF MY hair, and stepped up to Tanya's little home, and sighed. Tanya wanted a big house on a hill like my parents had and said that someday, she'd marry a man of means. Unfortunately, she hadn't been old enough to understand elves or what their idea of wealth was. Her parents were loving and kind, but they had passed just before Tanya turned sixteen.

I had helped her clean out the house and spruce it up in her own way. It shone with

Christmas magic just like our house seemed to.

At least until she met and broke up with her first boyfriend. Then the glow of her house faded. With each breakup, it seemed to get darker, and now as I stood studying the outer walls, I blinked at the almost black patches sticking out from beneath the sticking snow.

She deserved better than this.

I took a breath and pushed down the sadness that overtook me before I clanked the knocker against the door three times. When the door opened, my oldest friend peered out. Her eyes were ringed in red and her cheeks blotchy from crying.

"Chrissy?" She blinked as if trying to correct her vision. "What are you doing here?"

I shuffled my feet. "My dad thought you might need a friend." I offered her my best conciliatory smile. "And from the looks of you, I'm glad he called to let me know what was going on."

Tanya sniffled and opened the door for me to come in out of the storm. I slid inside, and she closed the door before leading me into the kitchen, where she busied herself with making me a hot chocolate.

"What happened?" I made myself comfortable at one of the stools lining the pristine island and focused on her, ignoring the nagging thought of the job back in the city.

"He said he didn't feel a connection with me." She let out a laugh before she slathered my cup with whipped cream. She slid it across the island and made one for herself, too.

"And you did?" I took a sip. It was good, but not as good as the ones I make at my parents.

She shook the whipped cream can but paused at my question as the cocoa machine spit out her drink into the cup. Then she started shaking the canister again. She didn't speak until her cup was adorned with what looked like half the container of cream. She slid into the seat next to me with a sigh.

"I don't know." She sipped the drink. "But it doesn't matter because there are no more eligible elves. I'm destined to be alone and bitter for the rest of my life." She sulked like a child and glanced at me. "How do you do it?"

I covered her hand with mine and raised an eyebrow. "Do what?"

"Live without someone to love?"

Oh. That. How do I find the words to explain that I didn't need a man in my life to Tanya, who thrived on that thought? It took me a moment to formulate the words so they wouldn't be offensive to her.

"I'm not interested in someone to take care of me. I'm just fine on my own. If someone crosses my path who can deal with monster hunting, then maybe I'd make a go of it. But it isn't a priority in my life." I squeezed her hand. "Besides, I love my parents and all the elves here at the North Pole."

"You've always been different that way." She took another sip of her drink. "You know what my Christmas wish was last year?"

I shook my head, but I could only imagine what someone so desperate for love would wish for.

"To find the love of my life." She let out an almost hysterical laugh. "I thought that was supposed to be Alvar."

I set my cup down and pulled her into a hug. "Well, maybe the love of your life isn't another person. Maybe it's something entirely different, like a calling."

After all, I loved my job, and the thrill of protecting someone against pure evil was all the rush I needed. Not that I hadn't dated. I had, but they were usually too self-absorbed or too damn clingy for me.

She hugged me back and then pulled away, wiping at the corners of her eyes.

I glanced at my watch, which was still set to New York time. I had a few hours before I had to be at the library for my next job.

"I actually can't stay much longer. I have a meeting with a client in a little bit."

Her chin quivered, and my chest squeezed at the sorrow cascading down her cheeks.

"Why don't you come to the city with me for a while?" I tried on a smile. "You can stay as long as you'd like. There are so many cool things I can show you in the city that you'll forget about Alvar in a New York minute. And maybe I'll even take you monster hunting with me if you promise not to get anywhere near me or Joy when I take the monster down. I'd hate to have my oldest friend turn to glitter."

She stared at me, and her eyes got wider and wider.

Outside, the storm seemed to calm.

"Are you serious?" she whispered.

The hope lighting up her face made me chuckle.

"Yes, I'm serious. It'll be nice to have company. And when I'm not working, I can show you all the cool spots to hang out. You never know, maybe you'll even meet the right guy."

I took a sip of the hot chocolate now that it had cooled a bit and studied her beautiful jewel-studded ears. The only time she'd get away with elf ears in the city were if there was a *Star Trek* convention, it was Halloween, or during the holidays.

"You'll need to glamour your ears, though. If it was winter, I'd just have you wear a beanie, but in the summer, that would be itchy and uncomfortable."

She touched the points of her ears self-consciously and glanced at mine. As a Kringle, I had human ears, not the delicate points like the elves.

"I can do that."

"So do you want to come with?"

She blinked rapidly, and then a smile as bright as the sunshine broke through the gloom around her. She put down her cup and clapped like a toddler being told they could have ice cream, and then she made a beeline to the stairs.

"I need to pack!"

Her exclamation traveled down the stairs, and I stared at my half-drained cup. I set it on the counter and followed her. I knew my friend's wardrobe. It was all flashy and skimpy like what she had on now. And every last piece screamed Christmas. That wouldn't do in the city. Especially in the summertime.

I got to her room just in time as she jammed fur-lined spandex pants into her bag.

"Um. It's like ninety-six degrees in the city right now. If you wear that, you'll melt."

She stood and waved at her current outfit. "What about this?"

Her outfit looked like some kind of Christmas bathing suit lined with fur and made to wear in a hot tub in Colorado Springs with a group of friendly guys, not something to wear in New York City in July.

I wrinkled my nose and shook my head. "Maybe we should stop at my folk's place on the way out. I have a few pairs of jeans and T-shirts there if my mother hasn't burned them for not being Christmassy enough."

Her expression fell, and she turned back to her closet filled with red and green, gold and silver, and everything so inappropriate for the summertime in the city.

"That stuff would be perfect for the winter," I said, trying to soften her pout. "But summers in the city can be brutal. Camisoles and shorts with flip-flops are the norm. If you're lucky enough to work inside, then pants work, but wandering the streets and even shopping trips…" I shook my head. "They all require the least amount of clothing as possible."

She waved at her outfit again and cocked an eyebrow. "This isn't a lot of clothing."

She had a point. "As cute as that is, it screams Christmas." My gaze dropped to her stylish furry boots. "And those, as nice as they are, are only going to make your feet sweat, and they'll get awfully smelly. Think how hot it usually is here this time of year." I started and began to riffle through what she had packed. "Well, add about thirty degrees to the temperature, and layer in beastly humidity. Then you have the city this time of year."

I pulled out things she had packed that were not summer worthy, piling them neatly on the bed as I went. She did have a couple sleeveless shirts that would work with shorts or a skirt this time of year, so I kept those. Beyond her undergarments, that's all that remained.

"Do you have exercise clothes?"

She smiled and crossed to her dresser. She pulled out cotton shorts and tank tops. Most were still in the green and red palette, but she did have some grey and black shorts too.

"Grab all of it. Do you have sneakers that you wear to work out?"

"Of course I do." She reached behind her flashy boots and pulled out a pair of red and gold sneakers. "I also have these." She showed me a black pair with silver etching.

"Both those will do."

"I also have a few pairs of yoga pants," she added and opened her bottom drawer.

Inside were an array of yoga pants, from plain to decorated with little reindeer.

I plucked out the more neutral ones and handed them to her to pack up. She would be well-dressed for the summer season now, however, she did lack some basic jeans, but that would be easily remedied by a trip to the store.

I walked by her closet again and stopped at something that caught my eye in the back. I pushed the frilly clothing aside and smiled at the black leather jacket. It looked similar to the one I wore once the cold set in over the city.

I pulled it out and turned to her, holding it up to my chest with a grin.

Tanya's cheeks went the color of her red skirt. "I've always liked yours, but never had the nerve to wear it in the village."

I handed it to her. "Pack it up. Sometimes it gets cold at night, and it's badass."

She didn't question me, and we looked at her bag, nearly stuffed to the brim.

"I just need my toothbrush and hairbrush, and I'll be ready to go."

"Change into one of the yoga pants and tank tops first." I reached into her closet and pulled out the least offensive boots I could find. A black leather pair that went mid-calf on Tanya. It would save her sneakers from getting soggy on the way to the portal.

"I need to stop off at the house and change." I couldn't wear the fur-lined clothing I had on right now. I would melt the moment we hit SoHo.

The sun had finally broken through the clouds outside her bedroom window, and I was sure my father was going to be pleased by the shift in the weather.

She reached for her scepter with the snow globe on top. The one she always carried with her, like Joy was usually with me.

"I don't know about bringing that."

It's not that it wasn't cool, but if anyone decided to steal it, or it broke, she'd be without the bulk of her power. Come winter, the weather wouldn't be guaranteed. After all, she was the one to bring on the snow.

She looked at the ornate walking stick. "If you want me to glamour my ears for any period of time, I'm going to need the magical boost. Besides, if someone tries to hurt us, I'll freeze them on the spot."

She grinned, looking a little too much like a maniac.

"Fine." I supposed I could store it in the locked cabinet that Joy was relegated to when I wasn't hunting.

She changed into the yoga outfit and slipped her toothbrush into one pocket and her hairbrush and accessories into another before she slung her bag over her shoulder. "This is going to be so much fun!"

Tanya nearly skipped next to me all the way to my parents' house. The sun glinted on the fresh snow, sending rainbow prisms through the air and some of the elves were braving the cold to start the tedious job of clearing out snow paths between their homes and the town center.

I caught the relief on their faces as they saw Tanya outfitted with more than an overnight bag on her shoulder and an outfit that didn't glimmer as much as she did on her frame.

I sighed and prayed this was the right thing to do. Otherwise, New York was in for some nasty weather.

CHRISTMAS WISH
CHAPTER 3

TANYA'S EYES WERE AS wide as the largest ornament on our Christmas tree as we stepped out of the portal. Her head tilted back to see the skyscrapers, and she gasped, dropping her gaze to me.

"This is overwhelming." She moved closer to me as if I could protect her from the onslaught of wonders.

"Glamour," I whispered and hooked my arm around her elbow, leading her toward my apartment.

The cool slide of her magic brushed against me, and the points on her ears disappeared. She gripped her magic stick as if it would fly away at any moment as we walked. Tremors cascaded through her with each step.

"Are you okay, Tanya?" I asked softly as we shuffled on the busy city sidewalks.

She nodded. "Just overwhelmed."

I forgot the symphony of sensations and the raw emotions that had hit me the first time I saw New York City from the ground. It had been impressive from the sky each Christmas, but being at ground level, it seemed massive and a bit intimidating.

"I guess I didn't prepare you for this." I smirked and glanced up at the buildings as we passed. "I won't leave you alone until you know your way around as well as you know Santa's village."

"That could take years," she whispered, and her wide eyes turned to me before bouncing back to all the people surrounding us.

I could see the nerves climbing inside her as the temperature around us dropped. "Relax. It will only take a few days to get you acclimated here. Most of the streets are numbered, so you just have to remember the number of the street we are on and then figure out if you are uptown or downtown. And Broadway runs from Time's Square all the way downtown. It's like a big rectangular grid with avenues going north to south and streets going east to west. Once you learn the major tourist attractions, you can pretty much navigate anywhere without too much of an issue."

I smiled, trying to calm her nerves. I didn't want a snowstorm in July. "And the shopping here is awesome."

And if I got this job today, I would be able to take her out and buy some decidedly New York stuff for her to have back home.

She laughed like I was off my rocker, and the way she clung to me made me take a deep breath and say a prayer for patience.

The rest of the walk was spent gawking at the people and the buildings. I smiled as her trepidation turned to enthusiasm and the coolness dissipated from around her.

"There are a lot of men in New York City," she whispered.

I couldn't help but laugh. "Maybe you'll get lucky."

I elbowed her and turned her down the street where my apartment was.

Once I got her up into my studio apartment, which was probably the size of her bedroom up north, she flopped down on the bed and just stared at the ceiling. Outside, sirens wailed and horns beeped. I'd learned to tune out the constant din, but Tanya flinched at every new sound.

She looked at me. "How can you stand all the noise?"

"It's gotten to be white noise in the background for me." I had been in the city for over ten years and could hardly remember those first nights here. "But in the beginning, I had to sleep with a pillow over my head."

"Then why did you stay?"

Good question.

I glanced outside the window. "This is where the monsters are."

It had been easy once that truth had sunk in. Up until this past Christmas, they seemed to be localized to this city.

I wondered if they'd moved on to another location but shook that thought out of my head. "It's where I am needed. Besides, you've seen my toy making skills."

She snorted laughter. "Your toys would have terrified even the most hardened criminals."

I cracked a smile. She wasn't wrong. My toys looked like something right out of a horror movie. My Jack-in-the-box looked like a mutilated Chucky, and even some of the elder elves screamed when he popped out.

"So, you understand my need for my own path, and this provided me some freedom away from home. And once a year, I get to protect my father. A little noise is a small price to pay." I waved to the window. "And now that you're here with me, I don't have to miss home quite so much."

Her smile faded. "You missed home?"

I nodded. "Just don't tell my mother. Otherwise, I'll never hear the end of it."

I rolled my eyes and started unpacking her things and making room in my drawers for her stuff.

My phone buzzed, and I pulled it from my back pocket. I read the text from my latest client and sighed. He wanted to meet earlier than expected, and on top of that, he'd changed locations on me. Instead of the library a few blocks away, he wanted to meet in Central Park by the skating rink.

I requested he send me a picture so I would recognize him in the crowd. At the library, I had specified a section to meet. I didn't want to just walk up to any stranger and ask if they were the ones who'd contacted a monster hunter. That wasn't my style.

I glanced at Tanya. "Sooo..." I took a deep breath. "My client wants to meet across town in fifteen minutes."

My phone dinged, and a picture came up. Mr. Stephenson was actually kind of cute, and he had half of my next paycheck with him.

Tanya looked around the little apartment, at her half-unpacked bag, and then at me. The conflict of stay or go crunched her features.

"Do you want to still come with me?" A part of me hoped she would decline the invite and stay in favor of unpacking and getting comfortable in this little place, especially since I hadn't vetted this client like I usually did, and that nagging sense inside me started pinging again.

She glanced down at her clothing. "Am I dressed properly?"

I scanned her yoga pants and tank top. She'd probably be more comfortable in a skirt or shorts, but we didn't have time to filter through her clothing to find something cooler.

I nodded. "You're fine."

She popped up from the bed with her scepter in her hand, and I plastered a smile on my face, pretending to want her to come along, even though that inner warning had turned into a wailing siren.

This felt like a really bad idea.

CHRISTMAS WISH
CHAPTER 4

TANYA'S EYES WIDENED INTO saucers of awe as we walked up Broadway toward Central Park. The shop window displays kept yanking her attention to the things highlighted in each presentation, but at least she didn't pull me in front of all the windows.

Of course, the jewelry displays were an entirely different story. She fawned over them and dragged me to a stop for each shiny creation.

By the time we reached the southern tip of the park, I was thankful to be free of shops hanging us up. As it was, all her small diversions had me running late. I wish I had taken the subway instead, but that would have freaked Tanya out even more than the towering buildings. And a cab ride was definitely a no-go. Not with how crazy the drivers in the city were.

"Say nothing when we meet my client," I said to her as we approached the park roller rink.

During the winter, this oval concrete center was flooded with ice, but during the summer months, rollerblades and roller skates prevailed.

Tanya nodded, gripping her staff like it would stave off anyone who tried to attack us, but her gaze was locked on the skaters.

I surveyed the area and then zeroed in on a dark-haired man standing by the concession stand. Bright eyes surveyed the incoming crowd with an expression of hope that died each time someone he deemed interesting walked past. He faced away from the rink, checking out everyone who came into his field of view. When his eyes landed on me, hope bloomed across his face but faded when his gaze moved to Tanya walking next to me.

I glanced at the photo on my phone, confirming that was my client. I approached him with Tanya trailing behind me.

"Mr. Stephenson?" I asked when we were a few feet away. The questioning tilt of his head nearly made me laugh.

"I thought you said you'd come alone?"

I crossed the minimal distance and stopped in front of him. "My cousin surprised me with a visit," I said. "And I didn't think you'd want me to reschedule."

The stranger's cobalt-blue eyes raked over the two of us and his lips pressed together.

"I'm not sure you are right for the job," he said after a moment.

He stuffed his phone in his pocket and turned to step away.

I needed this job despite the unease screaming in my bones. "There isn't anyone else who hunts monsters in the city."

Oh, there were other monster hunters, but no one as proficient as I was, or anywhere near New York City.

The stranger stalled. "I'm not even sure what it is," he said quietly.

His gaze kept moving to Tanya like something about her was magnetic. Maybe it was her scepter, or maybe it was the cute, non-summery outfit she sported, but his distraction with her scraped over my skin like a legion of ghosts, prickling my intuition.

"Why don't you explain while we walk?" I did not wish to discuss monsters while the general public could overhear.

I stepped next to him and waved toward the walking path.

He glanced at Tanya again but kept a moderate walking pace as he chewed on his lower lip. He appeared to be either in his late twenties or early thirties and fit with a lean form that seemed to be thrumming with angst.

With a sigh that could have mowed over a small bush, he said, "I don't know that it's a monster per se."

"You've already said that. Why don't you describe what is happening or what you've seen so I can make an assessment of whether it is critical to capture or kill said beast?"

He stopped and stared at me as if I had just committed the greatest of sins. "You kill them?"

I pointed to my chest. "Monster hunter. What did you think we did when we found them?"

"I don't know. Maybe set them free?" His voice squeaked as he led us to a more secluded area of the park.

The path was free of other people as if this area was off-limits to the public.

Tanya's gaze held the same trepidation as my potential client. I was sure neither of them had so much as killed a fly in their lifetimes. I ignored their combined indignation.

"Free them where? So they can terrorize someone else?" I shook my head. "There is no concept of monster jail anywhere on Earth. There isn't anything in the human realm that could cage one anyway."

He blinked so rapidly that I felt a breeze, and I wasn't even in his personal space.

I waved my hand in a circle, hoping it would coax more information out of him.

"It's probably the size of a medium-size dog and has the most hideous face I've ever seen, and its eyes were as red as a stop light."

"What color is it?"

"Greyish green?" His voice lilted with the question.

There were a few creatures that fell into his description. "Wings?"

He nodded, and his eyes flared with hope, as if I had all the answers.

My stomach dropped. The appearance of wings narrowed it down, and if it was what I thought, it would have to be doing someone's bidding because gargoyles only terrorized when ordered to.

"You wouldn't happen to have snapped a picture on your phone, would you, Mr. Stephenson?"

"No." He deflated before me. "And please call me Andrew. Mr. Stephenson reminds me too much of my father."

"Okay, Andrew, so what actually happened with this creature?" I scanned him, remembering the gargoyles that had attacked my father and me last Christmas Eve.

An attacking gargoyle was likely to leave marks, if you were lucky enough to escape. I didn't see any bandages visible, but then again, they went for the chest or abdomen to cause maximum pain.

Andrew glanced at me and then Tanya. "You're not going to question what I saw?"

I let out a soft chuckle and shook my head. "I've seen so many different things over the years. But what I need to know from you is exactly what happened."

He dropped his gaze to the ground. "It showed up when my ex and I were arguing, and she freaked out. The thing hissed at me and then chased after her."

"And was that the only time you saw the creature?"

"No. I saw her again, and the thing came at me, chasing me away this time."

I chewed my lower lip. Gargoyles were protectors, unless they were controlled by someone like what had happened last Christmas. What Andrew described was in line with their usual behavior when protecting someone. Which left me uncomfortable.

"What were you arguing about?" I asked, eyeing our remote location as he kept walking.

His entire demeanor shifted. "That's none of your business."

"Okay." I traded a glance with Tanya and then focused back on Andrew. "Why do you want the creature gone?"

"Because it won't let me get near her." His exasperation came through in his voice as well as his wild hand motions.

"But isn't she your ex?" Tanya asked before I could formulate my next thought.

She twirled a hair around her finger and smiled at Andrew.

He stared at her as if mesmerized. "Yes. She is my *ex*."

I did not like the flirty eyes he was giving Tanya. She responded in the same way, letting out a little giggle as if she were a schoolgirl.

Oh hell no.

The gargoyle was protecting his ex from him.

That did not bode well for his character, and from the look on Tanya's face, he was next on her list of revolving men. There was no way I was going to let her crawl into bed with this asshole.

"I'm not sure I can help," I said after a beat.

Andrew's gaze jumped to mine and was lined with irritation. "Why not?"

"The creature did not attack. What you described is their normal protective mode, not their attack mode. And trust me, I have seen them attack. Does the gargoyle have a reason to keep you from your ex?"

His eyes narrowed and his lips thinned. "I need you to get rid of it. Isn't that your job?"

"My job is to get rid of monsters. What you've described is not a monster." I shifted into a more defensive stance, putting myself between him and Tanya, and then raised my eyebrow to try to make my point.

"It won't let me even speak to her." His voice rose, along with a red hue that crept into his cheeks.

His reaction was enough to solidify my decision.

"And why is that? Why does a gargoyle feel compelled to protect her from you?"

Tanya gasped at my insinuation, and her eyes narrowed at Andrew as my words penetrated the flirty side of her. The temperature around us plummeted.

Andrew glared at me and then glanced up at the sky as goose flesh broke out on his arms. "I. Don't. Know."

I laughed and stopped walking, grabbing Tanya's wrist, halting her forward motion. Andrew took a step and then spun on us.

He pointed a finger from a tightly fisted hand. "You women are all alike," he snarled.

He stepped closer invading my space and puffing his chest out.

I stared up at him. "You really think your little macho act will intimidate me?" I pushed Tanya away in case this turned into a fist fight. "You better rethink your next move, Andrew."

My voice carried the chill that laced the air.

"And you better not lay a finger on my cousin, or I'll turn you into a human popsicle," Tanya said from behind me.

His gaze moved to her. "I bet she likes being slapped around."

"Walk away," I growled.

I wasn't sure if I was telling Tanya to go or Andrew, but my temper was just about to snap, and when I got mad, things usually got ugly. This asshat was made from the darker side of humanity, which made my hands itch. *He* was the monster, and just for a moment, I wished I had Joy on my back.

His hand shot out and grasped my throat, and in the next moment, his entire form was encased in ice.

Tanya slammed her cane down on his forearm, and his arm shattered into a million tiny pieces of ice, releasing me from his grip.

I rubbed my throat and stepped back before I spun and headed back in the direction of the apartment. There was no explanation as to why a human was now solid ice in Central Park. If he ever thawed, he'd come to without his forearm. I didn't want to be anywhere in the vicinity when that occurred.

My first stupid move was to bring Tanya; my second was not vetting this job to begin with.

CHRISTMAS WISH
CHAPTER 5

TANYA CAUGHT UP WITH me. "Are you angry?"

"Not at you." I took a breath as we made our way back to the more populated areas of the park. "Sometimes people can be the monsters, and it always throws me a little." I let out a high-pitched laugh. "Although, with the naughty list being a reality, you'd think I would have already accepted that."

We passed the subway entrance, and I considered taking Tanya down there, but after what she had done in the park, I didn't know if her freezing frenzy would extend to the stuffed subway. When Andrew was discovered, that would be quite the news story. If he didn't melt into a puddle of grossness first.

I chewed my lip. "I appreciate what you did back there for me, but you can't go freezing anyone who threatens us."

"He was the monster." She straightened her back. "And don't you stop monsters?"

I gave her a curt nod. "But I don't mess with humans." My voice was soft enough so she could hear me, but no one else around me could. I had to remember she was an elf and perhaps did not know the ramifications of messing with the human realm. "I usually leave that to human law enforcement."

"Oh."

The chill in the air draped over me, and I stopped and faced her, taking her free hand.

"Tanya, chill. We don't need a snowstorm in the middle of July here." I cocked an eyebrow at her.

"He would have hurt you," she whined as I moved her into a quiet alley.

"No. I would have schooled his ass and left him dazed on the sidewalk."

"How? He was choking you." Her wide eyes implored me to explain.

"I'm a black belt in a few different martial arts, and that sniveling idiot wouldn't have been the one who takes me down anyway."

"How can you be so sure? What if he has a different kind of magic? What if he poisoned you with his touch?" Her eyes got wider and wider with each question.

Before Tanya could ask another insane question, I smiled at her naïveté. "Humans don't possess magic the way the elves do."

Tanya gaped at me as if I had told her dragons and unicorns weren't real. "Are you sure?" she whispered.

Her eyes darted to the alley entrance where people moved about oblivious to our conversation.

"Yes. That is why we need to keep ours a secret here. If they found out, they'd want our magic and our freedom, and possibly even our very lives." I gently guided her back into the flow of human traffic heading toward mid-town.

She didn't window shop like she had before. Her brow was furrowed in thought all the way back to the apartment.

But the moment we were inside, she spun on me. "Why didn't you tell me there was no magic here? I wouldn't have used mine on that cute idiot."

Her eyes widened and she covered her mouth.

I smirked. "He was a little cute at first glance, but you dodged a bullet with that one. If his girlfriend is being protected by a gargoyle, he must be real nasty behind closed doors. They don't safeguard against just awful words, either."

At least that's what the gargoyle I cornered after the Christmas Eve fiasco had told me. He had been especially upset with what had happened to Santa and apologized for his species' actions, even though they were being controlled by dark magic. It was an enlightening conversation and one that gave me insight into gargoyles.

"And I didn't say there was no magic here. There is, but it's just not found in humans."

Tanya chewed on her lip, and took a seat on the bed that doubled as a couch. I busied myself with pouring some tortilla chips and a bowl of cheesy salsa and brought it to the coffee table to share with Tanya.

I switched on the television, and she gawked at it. I kept forgetting that she was from the North Pole and was going through some of the same wonders of the human world as I had my first few months in the city.

"What sorcery is this?" She waved her hand at the picture on the screen.

"It's called television." I pressed my lips together while I figured out a way to explain it that she would understand. "You know the annual play the elves put on every year?"

She nodded.

"Well, the people you see on the screen are actors like the elves in the play. Except they are being filmed, and then that movie or show that is taped is broadcast over the television."

Her eyes widened even more, and she scooted to the edge of the seat as the scene captured all her attention.

I leaned back in the chair, closing my eyes as I replayed the debacle in the park, and wondered what else could go wrong.

CHRISTMAS WISH
CHAPTER 6

A KNOCK ON THE door startled me.

I traded a glance with Tanya. There were very few people who visited me in my apartment. It was either the elderly neighbor looking for something I didn't stock in my kitchen, or my friend from the police force who came to me when things got weird.

With a frozen corpse in Central Park, it would probably be Ben, my trusty New York police department officer.

I opened the door and sighed as I met his green-eyed gaze. Ben Metcalf was one of the good guys who knew what I did for a living. Although, it did take him a while to accept it, and to stop investigating me.

His eyes shifted beyond me to Tanya on the couch, whose attention was still glued to the television. "Oh. You have company."

"My cousin." I stepped out into the hall because if he was indeed here because of the iceman, then I didn't need Tanya interjecting and announcing that she froze the idiot. "What can I do for you, Ben?"

He shifted on his feet and looked down at the faded carpeting in the hallway. "I don't want to interrupt your visit, but there's something that I think is right up your alley." He paused as if trying to formulate the words. "There's what appears to be a frozen body in Central Park."

My heart dropped into my stomach, and I had to hold down a burp of acid.

I swallowed and composed myself. "And?"

"And it's the middle of July. No one should be frozen solid during this kind of weather." His voice shook a little as if the scene had frazzled him.

"Won't he just melt?" I asked.

Ben rolled his eyes and took off his hat before he swiped his hand through his short, sandy-blonde hair. "That's the thing and why I'm here talking to the woman who hunts monsters for a living. My partner touched the ice, and now he's a human popsicle, too."

I cocked an eyebrow at this new development. Especially since it had to do with Ben's elusive partner, whom I had yet to meet, and Ben and I had been friends for a solid two years at this point. An as far as I knew, when Tanya froze someone, it didn't spread to others.

Tanya opened the door and looked at me before she turned to Ben. She blinked as if waking from a long sleep and then licked her lips. At least she didn't have her scepter with her. The slow smile that appeared made her look more like the big bad wolf than an interested elf.

"Hello." Her delivery was laced with sensuality, and the air sizzled between the two of them. "Aren't you going to introduce me?"

"Ben, this is my cousin, Tanya. Tanya, this is Ben. A police officer here in New York City."

At least we had some semblance of a police force in the North Pole. Of course, their idea of a jail was the lap of luxury in comparison to a New York City precinct cell.

Ben nodded his head in respect. "Ma'am," he said in a rough voice I had never, in all the time I had known him, heard before.

If he had ever used that tone with me, our one date might have turned into something more than just friendship. Unfortunately, we never got past the friendship zone. Not with his skepticism of the monster realm. Which I cured him of when we came face-to-face with a Gashadokuro who was terrorizing a portion of Manhattan near where the World Trade Center fell. While the over-zealous skeleton wasn't necessarily a monster, it was stalking and killing people, and as such had to be put down.

"Ben was here about a frozen man in the park." I stared down Tanya, praying that she got my keep-your-mouth-shut expression. "And it seems anyone who touches the frozen human *also* freezes."

Her gaze slashed to mine and widened as if she understood her circumstances.

But then she opened her mouth. "That's never happened."

Shit. "Of course. It's not supposed to happen, especially at this time of year. It's the middle of summer, and too damn hot out to freeze anything."

I laughed, but it sounded unnatural and a bit desperate to me as I tried to cover up her slip.

But Ben barely even glanced my way.

His eyes were locked with Tanya's in a way that was almost enchanted. It was like a lost puppy found, and I thought I would have been more comfortable interrupting them doing the nasty right here on the hallway floor instead of seeing the longing in his eyes that matched hers.

Could Ben be the one for Tanya? That would be a hell of a coincidence, and so not good considering the circumstances.

He extended his hand toward Tanya as if the reason he was here had completely escaped his mind. "Ben Metcalf."

"Tanya Snow," she said and smiled.

The color in her cheeks bloomed pink, and she reached out to take his hand.

The minute their skin touched, light filled the hallway, binding the two together in a way that made my stomach plummet. I had seen soulmates find each other before, and my father said only a Kringle could see the magic that connection puts out. It always amazed me.

No wonder she couldn't find her perfect partner up in the North Pole. He was here in New York City all this time.

But when he found out she was the cause of the frozen man in the park, their short-lived connection would certainly shatter the way the asshat's arm had when she smashed it with her staff.

I cleared my throat, and Tanya pulled her hand away from his. Sparks seemed to fill the air between them, but they both looked at me as if remembering where they were.

Ben blinked and glanced at his hand before shoving it into his pocket. He seemed to shake himself back to the here and now as he focused on me.

"Do you think this is something you can look into?" His voice cracked.

"I can look into it."

He gave me a curt nod and then swung his gaze toward Tanya. "I'll stop back after my shift. If you go down to check out the scene, please don't breach the police tape. We wouldn't want anyone else hurt."

His soft smile aimed at Tanya clenched my stomach. But she was seeing too many stars to hear what he was saying.

"It was a pleasure meeting you," he said as he stepped backwards.

"Likewise."

I pushed her back in the apartment before she said anything else and closed the door on Ben's lingering stare. The solid wood between them broke the spell.

"I felt something when our hands touched that I've never felt before. Why did you send him away?" Her hands slammed into her hips, and her eyes narrowed at me.

My breath frosted in the chill Tanya created. "Because he will throw you in jail for killing that idiot and now his partner. If it was just my client, then that would be justifiable, but your freezing of him extended to a police officer." I pointed at the door. "Ben's partner."

Tanya blinked quickly, and her mouth popped open. "I froze him. I didn't kill him."

I wiped my face and took a breath. I had to remember she had been in Santa's village in the North Pole for her entire life. There, if you freeze an elf, they eventually thaw or break out of the ice and are fine. But I didn't think cryogenics was all that advanced in the human world.

I wasn't sure if humans would react the same as an elf.

As much as the image of Andrew's arm shattering in my head haunted me, I asked anyway, "Can you reverse what you did?"

She stared at me as if I'd just asked her to give birth to the next Messiah, but before she could speak, my phone rang out with "Santa Claus is Coming to Town."

Shit. We didn't need my father to weigh in on this debacle.

CHRISTMAS WISH
CHAPTER 7

"WHAT HAPPENED?" MY FATHER demanded the moment I answered.

It was as if he knew something terrible had occurred.

The room darkened with his words, and I met Tanya's gaze and then focused on the window beyond her. The sky had gone from a crisp blue to a smokey grey like that of a storm was rolling through.

I covered the phone with my hand. "Are you doing that?"

"Doing what?"

I pointed to the window, which now had frost creeping around the edges, and beyond the pane, the first hint of snow streaked the air.

Tanya shook her head. "I-I don't think so."

She spun back in my direction with wide eyes. Tanya didn't unintentionally start storms unless she was super upset.

"Chrissy!" My father's sharp admonishment came over the phone.

"I am not sure what's going on, Dad." I couldn't tell him nothing was happening, because I didn't lie well, and everything in his tone cast knowledge of our precarious situation. "We went to the park to meet a client, who turned out to be a real dickhead, and when he attempted to choke some sense into me, Tanya froze him."

My father blew out a stream of air that sounded like a blizzard on the other end of the phone. "You took Tanya to New York with you?"

I bristled at his dark tone. "Yeah. I thought it would be a nice diversion for her."

"Damn it, Chrissy. Elves should not be in the human world."

"You had Bernard riding with you for years on the sleigh." I didn't know what my father was getting at, and his angry attitude put me on the defensive.

"He was on the sleigh. Protected by Christmas magic." My father's sigh followed. "She used her magic?"

"Yes. She froze an idiot with her scepter when he started to choke me."

"You let her bring her snow globe staff there?"

"Yes. That's what she used to freeze the guy."

"Good God," he muttered.

"I use Joy all the time. What's the big deal?"

"Even though Joy was made with elf magic, you wield it. You are not an elf, Chrissy." His exasperation came over the phone line clearly. "I think I need to come to the city before you two cause any further damage."

"I can handle it." I allowed this mess. It was mine to clean up. "We're going down to the crime scene so Tanya can unfreeze the idiot."

"What's done cannot be undone, Chrissy. Tanya's magic unleashed something dark and dangerous in the human realm. It's why no elves have set foot there since this being was banished. It's something I had hoped would never be unleashed. I did not think you would bring her to the city with you."

Damn it.

"You should have told me about this thing, Dad." I moved my gaze to the brewing storm outside. "Does this thing freeze anything it touches?" My trepidation rang in my voice. "Or anyone who touches it?"

Silence filtered over the line before he said, "The parasite manifests the magic that set it free."

Oh great. Tanya was the frost queen. She could freeze and thaw and cause a blizzard with any emotional outburst.

"What are we dealing with?" I put the phone on speaker, grabbing a pen and paper as I reverted to the monster hunter because that was the safest option right now.

"A demonic parasite who I banished millenniums ago. It's how I earned this job and my immortality. Now that it has been unleashed, all we know and love is in danger. Earth. The North Pole. Christmas. Everything." He took a breath. "And you cannot use Joy on this beast now that it's been unleashed. It will deplete the sword of its magic and leave you vulnerable. Same with you, Tanya. You cannot bring the scepter into the open. Whatever magic you used to freeze that man is gone. It will never be replenished so long as that thing lives."

"I still feel the magic, though." She had picked up her scepter as we spoke and was inspecting the snow globe.

"You didn't use all your magic on him, but whatever you expended woke this demonic parasite. And usually, your magic will regenerate back to full strength. But not this time. This time it's just gone, and that thing will be hunting you to take the rest of your magic, and not just what your staff holds. The parasite will deplete the magic you hold in each one of your cells."

"What about those it has already frozen?" Tanya asked, meeting my gaze with her horrified one. "Are they just as lost as what magic I used?"

"If we prevail, they'll survive. If we die, they'll die alongside us."

"What about her glamour?" I wasn't sure what would happen if I brought Tanya out in the open with her elf ears.

"Tanya should not leave the apartment at this point. The demon has tasted her magic and will be looking for her to drain the rest of it."

"Should I send her home, then?"

"No. If any of the static portals open, that thing could get through, and then it's not just New York that's in jeopardy."

"Then how are you going to get here?" Tanya asked.

I let my lips tilt into a smile. My father had the ability to create portals anywhere. That wasn't common knowledge either.

His chuckle bled through the line. "I can create a portal on the fly."

Wind picked up around the living room, and a moment later, my father stepped onto the worn carpet of my little apartment. I stared at him wearing jeans and a leather jacket and a clean-shaven face. His white hair was slicked back as if he had just stepped out of the shower.

He looked nothing like Santa Claus. But what gave me a start enough so that I had to do a double take were the number of knife holders attached to each of his thighs, along with ornately carved wooden handles sticking out of each one.

"Really?" I waved at his get up.

"My magic is safeguarded with your mother. When I'm ready to go back home, I just need to signal her, and she'll open a portal for me."

My heart bottomed out. I had never known my father not to have that magical twinkle about him, and the gravity of the situation hit.

He was not dressed for summer in the city, but considering the snowstorm howling outside, perhaps he was dressed appropriately.

He raised an eyebrow at me. "Suit up." He pointed at Tanya. "And you stay put."

I grabbed my jeans and a black tank top and headed in the direction of the bathroom to change.

A fist banged on my door, and we all spun in that direction.

"Chrissy?"

Ben's voice penetrated the wood, and I opened the door before my father could ask any questions.

"Everything in the city is freezing..." he started.

His eyes were wild and overly large as if he couldn't grasp the reality around him. It was the same look he'd had when he first saw the Gashadokuro. The minute his gaze moved beyond me, he stopped talking and just blinked at the sight of my father.

"Chris Kringle." My dad extended his hand. "I am Chrissy's father."

Ben stared, and then his gaze bounced to mine and back again. "Um. Ben Metcalf. Detective Ben Metcalf. Sir."

He shook my father's hand.

My dad looked at me and cocked his eyebrow.

"Ben comes to me when things out of the ordinary are taking place. He knows what I do."

"Ah. Well, go get changed, and make sure you don't have any magical weapons. Then let's go get this thing."

"Do you hunt monsters like Chrissy?" Ben asked just as I slid into the bathroom.

"Not usually."

I closed the door as Ben's eyebrows shot up at my father's answer.

I quickly stripped my yoga pants, and pulled on my jeans, and then changed my shirt, wondering just how the conversation between my father and Ben was going to go. It was one of the quickest wardrobe changes that I've ever done and I opened the door to Ben's narrowed gaze.

My father glanced at me as I strode out of the bathroom and slipped into my black boots that complemented my leather jacket. I reached for my knife holders and started clasping them on my thighs. The familiar weight of my weapons gave my unsteady nerves some steel to cling to.

Then my father turned to Ben. "Please stay with Tanya and keep her safe."

"I'm sorry, but I don't take orders from you."

"You do if you want that boat for Christmas."

"Excuse me?"

"Yamaha 275SE, if I'm not mistaken." He ran his finger along the side of his nose and winked.

I straightened just in time to catch the twinkle that escaped from my father's eye and lit up the room. Ben's eyes had widened enough to give Tanya's first look at the city a run.

"How does he know that?"

Now, I'm not psychic, but I would bet a thousand dollars that was what Ben was thinking. But since he was in the middle of this fiasco, he had a right to know exactly who he was dealing with.

"He's a Kringle." I raised and lowered my shoulder.

After a moment, his eyes widened. "Chris Kringle, like in Santa Claus?" His voice cracked.

My father grinned and managed to do the same nonchalant shrug I'd don a few seconds ago. He didn't exactly confirm Ben's question aloud, but the way Tanya grinned and nodded from behind him sealed the answer.

Ben turned to me. "Are you kidding me?"

"We need to go. Can you please stay with my cousin?" I pointed in Tanya's direction.

"Is she really your cousin?" Ben's narrowed eyes screamed suspicion.

I sighed. He deserved the truth.

"She's my oldest and dearest friend from home. I'll let her explain. We need to go fix this." I waved at the July snowstorm raging outside and then met Tanya's gaze. "Please do not leave this apartment, no matter what happens. Okay?"

Tanya glanced at the storm and then at Ben before she nodded. "I'm sorry."

"It isn't your fault," my father said. "I should have let Chrissy know what the consequences of letting anyone from home coming here were. That was my mistake."

Ben raised an eyebrow.

"I'll explain when we get back." I sent my most reassuring smile their way, and my father and I stepped into the hallway.

"*If* we get back," my dad said softly as we headed toward the stairwell and the winter storm beyond.

CHRISTMAS WISH
CHAPTER 8

"I HAVEN'T EXPERIENCED THIS kind of weather since the blizzard of '78." My father leaned into the icy wind as we marched uptown toward the place things had gone sideways—Central Park.

The sidewalks were unusually barren of foot traffic, and a few cars headed uptown, but nothing traveled south on the road. It was eerie. I didn't remember New York City ever being this quiet.

"I wish we had the reindeer," I muttered.

They knew how to fly through a storm like this.

My dad chuckled. "I hear you. But this war is no place for them."

"War?" I gave my father a side eye while trying to protect my face from the ice pelting it.

"Yes. This is a war against evil. What we are fighting is equivalent to the devil himself. And this time, we have to do more than just banish the beast." He traded a glance with me that sent a chill all the way to the bone. "And to do that, we will have to kill the human host it has possessed before it can skip out of the body."

Oh, great. I was the best at hunting monsters, but hunting and killing a higher demon possessing a person sounded awfully harrowing. But I couldn't imagine losing. Not with all that was at stake, including my father's life.

It wasn't Christmas, so I didn't have access to any of the magic that had resurrected my father from nearly dying on Christmas Eve. No matter how much I wished for more, I knew my magic was limited to two days a year—Christmas Eve and Christmas Day.

"What's our plan?"

"Survive and decapitate the bastard."

I snorted a laugh that quickly died as we turned the corner onto Broadway.

I blinked at the spectacle a few blocks ahead. Nothing moved. We had to weave through the frozen bodies on the sidewalk and occasionally step onto the slick street to make our way through.

The cars were encased in ice just like the people. Whatever froze them had stalled every engine. Nothing around us moved, and the only noise besides our feet scraping on ice and snow was the wind howling down the avenue.

I wondered how close to this creeping line of snow and ice Ben had gotten before he escaped being another casualty.

Then a thought filled my heart with dread. Ben had been at ground zero with this parasite.

"Dad, you don't think the demon got into Ben, do you?"

My father slowed for a moment and looked over his shoulder. He swallowed hard and then shook his head. "No. He would have syphoned Tanya's magic the moment he stepped in the apartment. I guess his knowledge of monsters may have saved him. He's just smart enough to see this and run." He waved at the spectacle around us.

"Good. Because I think he's Tanya's destined match." I side-eyed him to see his reaction. "I saw the soul connection when they shook hands."

I caught the appearance of dimples before my father schooled his expression.

I narrowed my gaze. "You knew her match was here in the human realm?"

"I knew he was not in the North Pole, but I had no idea how to help them find each other." He traded a glance with me. "Did you know both their wishes last Christmas were to find 'the one'?"

I knew that had been Tanya's wish, but I would have never guessed that Ben would have wished that too. He'd never expressed that he was lonely. At least not to me.

"I couldn't have arranged this. Not without plucking a poor soul from the human realm and bringing him back to the North Pole," my father continued. "There's a power much higher than mine in play, and I'm not sure if your decision to bring her here facilitated the match or not, but I'll gladly take some of the glory for a Christmas wish coming true." His ghostly smile disappeared. "I just hope they get to enjoy that wish."

"I do, too."

We kept moving forward through the frozen landscape.

"Why aren't we affected by this?" I waved at our surroundings and the icy wind pelted my skin. I shoved my hand back into my pocket.

"We are Kringles." He chewed on his lip as we trudged through a new layer of snow coating the streets.

I shivered at the sheer number of souls that could be lost if we didn't win. "How far will this go if we can't stop it?"

"It will go until it finds the source of magic that awakened it."

I glanced over my shoulder. The freeze had started a little over six blocks away from my apartment, and it looked like more of the road was encased in ice, but I couldn't tell with all the wind and snow whipping around us.

"We should have sent her and her scepter back to the North Pole."

My father's gaze was locked in front of us, and I turned my attention uptown. The likeness of Andrew Stephenson stood in the center of Times Square like some grade-school bully. His frozen stump pointed at me as if I were the one who had caused this chaos in my city.

The only difference between the asshole in the park and this new version on the street was his sheer mass. He was easily ten times the size he had been when Tanya froze him. He now reached up two or three floors on the buildings surrounding us.

Andrew lowered his stump. The demonic parasite had given Andrew's frozen form animation.

"Abaddon." My father's growling voice pulled my attention to him.

That was a name I had heard. Albeit on a television show.

Andrew grinned. "Saint Nick. I cannot wait to destroy you."

"I can't wait to see you try."

Andrew's icy stare pinned on me. "When every street in this city is covered with your father's blood, and I have his head as a new hood ornament on his sleigh, you will become my slave to atone for what you did to my host's body."

He waved his stump and then grinned in a salacious way.

It was enough to make me shiver, and for the first time in my life, a chill settled in my bones.

"And I will be sure to give you a front-row seat to the destruction of this world."

I shrugged off the chill and reached for the hilt of my knives. "I don't think so."

My father pulled out his blades, too. "Just be mindful of where I am," he said, low enough to almost be drowned out by the wind.

Before we could take a step forward, a half-dozen icicles flew our way. I spun out of the way, slapping a couple of them to the ground with my knives.

My father grunted once. I snapped my gaze to him. One of the ice shards was embedded in his thigh, but the rest were broken on the ground around us.

He limped forward, snarling at the demon, and while their attention was focused on each other, I aimed and threw one of my blades towards the monster's heart.

The bastard pivoted enough so my knife missed his heart, but it did sink into his side. He roared so loudly that the snow shattered into fine bits in the air that stung with the gale force winds.

I quickly drew another one of my knives. I didn't want either hand to be empty when we closed the distance.

While Andrew dug the knife out of his side, my father took the opportunity to wrap his scarf around his thigh above where the icicle still penetrated his skin. He tightened it and then continued his slow trek forward.

I kept my pace equal to his since I did not want to leave him vulnerable.

Andrew's gaze locked in the direction of my apartment, and his smile spread. "I know where the rest of this magic is."

He cast the knife aside and started toward us, stretching his good hand out to blast us with ice and snow.

We held our ground until what could only be categorized as a tribal war cry came from behind us. Wind just as strong as what Andrew was sending at us hit our backs, keeping us locked between the two forces.

I glanced over my shoulder to see Tanya striding toward us. Her face was as red and angry as I'd ever seen, and her gaze was zeroed in on the form of Andrew.

What dropped my heart into the pit of my stomach was her staff gripped in her hand.

We were totally screwed.

CHRISTMAS WISH
CHAPTER 9

"YOU FROZE MY SOULMATE!" Her scream shattered the air over the asphalt, cracking car windows with her volume.

She pointed her scepter at Andrew.

I wanted to tell her to hide it, or to run, but there was no reasoning with the rage in her eyes.

"You want this?" She shook the staff at him.

He grinned and sent a smug look in my father's direction. "This may be much easier than I thought."

He chuckled in a gleeful manner, but his expression changed to that of utter horror.

I turned back to Tanya just in time to see her swing the scepter toward the ground with the force of an avalanche. The sound it made when it hit the road was equal to the shrill scream coming from Andrew. The scepter shattered into ash.

"Not in my lifetime," she growled just as her power exploded into the stratosphere, out of reach of Andrew's dark host.

Tanya had given up her magic. Willingly.

The explosion knocked me to the ground, and I lost one of my knives on impact. My father sprawled next to me with a pained groan. I scrambled across the snow to grip the knife that had skidded away and glanced up at Times Square.

The blast had also tossed Andrew into the air as whatever magic was in the vicinity was sucked out of him. Tanya's sacrifice had been more powerful than this demonic parasite.

Andrew's shadow fell onto the bandstand, and he followed, shrinking back to human form before he landed. Still, the force of his fall cracked the stands, dropping him to the ground in a flurry of metal and plastic. He was now nearly our size, which would make this fight much more even rather than if we had had to fight the towering menace.

We still had to end him before he body-jumped though.

Tanya reached us and helped my father to his feet, and then she offered me a hand. Her ears poked out of her hair now that her magic had been shattered along with her scepter.

"Do you have an extra one of those?" She pointed at the knives in my hand.

I offered her the one that had slid on the pavement, and the three of us advanced toward the broken bandstands with the same intent written on our faces.

Destroy the monster.

Andrew rose from the wreckage with a metal rod from the broken bandstand in his hand. His pallor was less arctic than before, and his stump seemed to be weeping blood through a thin layer of ice. It was as if whatever was animating his body was melting. But his eyes still held deadly determination.

We came within hitting distance, and Andrew swung. Both Tanya and I evaded the hit, but the rod connected with my father's shoulder, sending him to the ground.

Before Andrew could reverse his swing and clock my father again, Tanya leaped forward, swinging her knife like she was pitching a curveball, and she screamed like a possessed banshee.

Surprise flitted over Andrew's face as Tanya collided with his shoulder, but her arm kept moving with brute force around the front of him. Blood drizzled from his ear as if her scream had shattered his eardrum, but it was the widening of his eyes that brought forth my satisfaction.

My friend had gone feral enough to kill, and not just freeze, another being and I wasn't going to leave this all to her. Her soft heart would regret killing, even if it was necessary to bring her soulmate back from the deep freeze that had captured the city around us.

I jumped in and buried my knife into his back, directly in line with his heart. Metal scraped across metal, and I met Tanya's gaze over Andrew's shoulder. Her blade had punctured his heart from the front, and mine from the back. But in order to actually do the damage, the blades had to be removed.

I pulled mine out and smiled at the black blood coating the knife. If that didn't kill this bastard, we were totally screwed.

Tanya did the same, and the pipe fell from Andrew's hand, clattering onto the ground. He teetered on his feet.

My father gently moved Tanya out of the way and pulled out a knife with an extra-long blade from his belt. With a forceful growl I didn't think possible from my father, he swung, slicing Andrew's head clean off. The dead body crumbled to the ground at our feet.

Then my father stumbled.

I moved, but Tanya was quicker, catching my father before he collapsed to the ground. The world around us blinked back into motion as if it had never been frozen.

Unfortunately, the transition was instantaneous, and we had a dead body at our feet, a mangled bandstand in front of us, and knives with the dead man's blood in our hands.

CHRISTMAS WISH
CHAPTER 10

"FREEZE!" A DEEP VOICE full of authority yelled from behind us. "Raise your hands where I can see them."

We did as we were instructed. All three of us lifted our arms into the air, still clasping the bloody knives.

"Drop your weapons."

"It would have been nice if he had asked us to do that first," my father muttered as he moved his hand to the side far enough away from his body not to be impaled when he dropped his knife.

We did the same, and the clang of metal on the concrete sounded oddly loud considering the shuffling of feet around us. New Yorkers didn't usually stop for anything, but they certainly gave this spectacle a wide berth.

Backup officers arrived quickly, and we were cuffed, and then hauled down the street to the Midtown South Precinct, and shoved into separate interrogation rooms.

Thankfully, they came in and removed my cuffs and gave me a disposable cup of water while I waited to be grilled. They left me stewing for long enough to make me irritable. My brain tumbled through all the scenarios that could play out, and the only one that truly made sense was being honest, even though it might open the door to some closely held truths.

A PLAIN-CLOTHED OFFICER stepped into the room. He looked just as tired as I felt and his peppered hair was spiked in places as if he had ran his hand through it multiple times. I'm sure he had been drilling my father for information all this time, and from the looks of him, he didn't get the information he desperately wanted.

All I needed to do was stick to the facts. The truth was the only thing that would exonerate us.

And our truth was really hard to swallow for those who did not believe in magic.

He took a seat and organized his notebook and pen before his grey-blue eyes looked up at me expectantly. "Start by telling me who the two people with you are."

"The man is my father, and the elf is my best friend from the North Pole."

He ran his hand down his face. "If you don't level with me, things will start to get very hard for you."

"Are you charging me with a crime?" I crossed my arms.

"We have tampering with a crime scene and mutilating a dead body. Plus, we have messages from his phone to yours." He waited a beat. "What is your relationship to the deceased?"

I tilted my head and narrowed my eyes. "We did not tamper with a crime scene. And if you have his text messages, then you know he was a potential client."

"Were you in the park this morning?"

I nodded. I could not reveal that Tanya had frozen him and started a near apocalypse. So, I gave him as much of the truth as I could without incriminating her. "Yes. I met my client at the skating rink, and after his explanation of what he wanted, I declined, and left him on the walking path, and came straight home."

"How did he end up frozen like a popsicle?"

I put my hands out in an overly animated shrug. "We didn't tamper with a crime scene," I repeated, just because I needed to divert his attention to something else.

He slammed his palm onto the table, making me startle. "Then how the hell did that frozen man get from Central Park to Times Square, and why did your knives have his blood on them? And what the hell happened to the others who had been frozen in the park?"

"We didn't move him from the crime scene in Central Park. And I have no idea what you mean by others." I furrowed my brow, giving him my best confused look.

After all, I only knew about Ben's partner. I didn't know about anyone else being human popsicles before the rest of the city was frozen by that demon bastard.

Besides, I couldn't very well tell the officer that Andrew had walked to Times Square and implicate us in a murder charge. I was already on thin ice with him.

WE hadn't moved Andrew from Central Park. He'd done that all on his own. We'd just stopped his frozen aspirations.

But the police weren't going to buy that. To them, no time had passed between the moment before they froze to a blink after they thawed, although the clock on the wall reflected the right time of day.

A thought jumped into my head then.

The freezing of the city had not actually stopped time. So, these people lost that time.

Just before I opened my mouth to enlighten this officer, the door opened, and someone appeared with a gold badge that contrasted with the silver badge hanging out of the interrogations officer's pocket.

"Banner, a word?" the senior officer asked, and then his gaze slid to mine.

I caught a mixture of confusion and awe in his eyes. It made my skin itch.

"Excuse me a moment." Banner stood, blocking my view of the senior officer.

The door closed behind him, and I leaned back in the chair, running my hands through my hair. At least I wasn't chained to the desk like a common criminal, but our situation was precarious at best.

When the door opened again, the senior officer stepped into the room with a coffee cup in one hand.

"I'm Captain Romano." He crossed and offered me his free hand in a friendly manner.

I hesitated, searching his gaze before I accepted his handshake. "Chrissy Kringle."

He tried to hide his scoffing laugh under his breath but didn't do a very good job of it. "It seems there are a couple officers here from the Central Park Precinct, one of whom had been previously frozen in the park, but seems to be perfectly unaffected now. They vouch for you and your friends."

"My father and my best friend," I clarified.

They were much more than friends. They were family.

He cleared his throat. "Yes. Well. The problem is, we have a dead and decapitated body blocks away from where that citizen had been frozen. And no logical explanation from any of you."

"That's because there is no logical explanation." Not in the human world anyway. It was perfectly logical in my mind.

"And are you always armed to the hilt when you go out on the streets of New York?" He pressed his lips together waiting like he expected me to screw up or something.

"When hunting monsters, yes."

He blinked a few times at me. I didn't think he expected me to answer that way.

"Monsters like..." He rolled his hand, prompting me to continue.

"Enchanted gargoyles, perytons, Gashadokuros, abominable snowmen, ghosts, ancient demonic parasites... You know, any monster that wreaks havoc here." I didn't know exactly how to describe Andrew beyond the way my father had, but I did my best.

The way he squinted at me, I knew he thought I was bullshitting him.

"You can ask Officer Metcalf about the Gashadokuros. He has firsthand experience with that one, as well as what I do for a living. Do I need to expand more?" I crossed my arms.

"What *do* you do for a living?"

"I hunt monsters. You can find me on the internet." I had a website and everything. It was how Ben tracked me down, and unfortunately how Andrew did as well.

"So, let's say for giggles I had a ghost problem?"

The captain was reaching. I could see it in his eyes. He wanted to pin a lot of things on my shoulders to make this a clean case. But it just wasn't all neat and tidy like he wanted it to be.

"You'd look me up online, contact me through my web form, and we would have a conversation."

He leaned forward. "What kind of conversation?"

"One in which I needed to know if the ghost was a true menace or just an inconvenience. I would ask you to detail what the ghost was doing. If it was simply moving things around, it just wants to be acknowledged. That is not what a monster hunter is called in for. But on the other hand, if it is hurting people, that's when I intervene and send it on its way."

"And how do you do that?" He took a sip of his coffee.

"Usually with Joy. My enchanted sword. It turns them into glitter."

He choked on the drink, coughing and sputtering while he cleared his lungs. "Excuse me?"

I just smiled at him. "My sword turns monsters into glitter."

"How come that man didn't turn to glitter, then?"

Oh, he thought he was so smart. But I was two steps ahead of him.

"Because I could not bring my magical sword to fight a demonic being who siphons magic." It was time to bring up the thought I'd had earlier before he interrupted my interrogation. I leaned forward and narrowed my gaze. "Tell me, Captain Romano, how do you account for everyone's time loss today?"

I used finger quotes around the words "time loss" to make my point.

He blinked at me and sat back in his chair.

"I imagine there was probably somewhere between two and four hours of missing time from everyone around here that no one can account for. One minute, it was a little before eleven in the morning, and then bam." I glanced at the clock over the door. "It's around three-thirty in the afternoon. Of course for some people, it may have been a little longer, depending upon how close or how far they were from the park. That would affect the amount of missing time. But for all of you, it's just gone."

His face paled as I spoke, and I leaned back slowly to let the truth sink in.

"For some, like that officer in the park, it's a bit more." I nodded toward the door. "Go on. Talk to your other officers or the front desk person or whoever and ask if they had some weird time slip in their day, too."

"And why would I do that?"

"Because every last one of you was frozen like that officer in the park."

He laughed as if I were insane.

"You do remember the snowstorm coming out of nowhere, right?"

His laughter faltered.

"Snow. In July." I pressed him further as doubt painted his features.

"Yes. It *was* snowing." He nodded, and the crease between his eyes deepened. He looked at his watch and then at the door. "I'll be right back."

I wondered what my father and Tanya were saying, and I hoped it was along the same lines. The truth, as bizarre as it sounded saying it out loud, would be the key to our freedom. And if Ben somehow explained he'd come to me for help before the ice creep got to him, then that would further solidify our story.

When the captain came back in the interrogation room, he looked much more frazzled. As if the curtain that had been drawn over his eyes had suddenly vanished. He sat and opened his mouth but closed it again before he wiped his face.

"Everyone has the time lapse, don't they?"

His eyes sharpened on me. "What did you do, some sort of mass hypnosis?"

"We stopped the end of civilization."

His bark of a laugh filled the room. "You, Santa Claus, and an elf stopped the end of the world."

"If you aren't careful, you'll end up on the naughty list." I smirked.

"Santa doesn't have a beard."

His defensive snap made me smile wider. "It's summer. A beard is itchy even in the North Pole."

"Argh!" He threw his hands up in the air. "Did you three rehearse this?"

I let my smile fade. "Speaking of my dad... Did anyone look at his leg?"

"Did you stab him, too?"

"No. That was one of several dozen icicles that the monster threw at us."

"And yet you don't have a scratch."

"No, I dodged them better than he did. But I'm sure you'll find a dent or two on my blades. Is he patched up?"

He shifted in his seat and glanced at the one-way mirror before he nodded. He stared at the table, chewing on his lower lip.

When he looked up again, he asked, "What would you do in my shoes?"

"If you need more facts to support what we are saying, go outside of the police station and ask about time loss. Ask the news stations here in Manhattan. There have to be anomalies out there. Not just with time loss, but the city itself becoming a winter landscape in seconds. I'm sure The Weather Channel was all over that. The rest of the world wasn't affected yet. So do your research, and then if you still find us guilty of something, book us. Otherwise, let us go."

He wiped his face. "I can't get past the Santa Claus part."

"Forget who my father is, and check the facts about the last six hours here in Manhattan. Then we can discuss your disbelief in miracles."

He seemed uncertain again as if I were testing the fabric of his very sanity. "That will take time."

I hiked my heels onto the table. "I've got the time."

He looked at the mirror behind me and then nodded before standing.

"Could you bring me a water and a PowerBar of some sort to tide me over?" I asked before he stepped out of the room.

He gave me a curt nod and closed the door.

I leaned back in the chair and tilted my head so I could see the mirror. "I'm telling the truth," I said to the people beyond my reflection.

And then I lowered my legs and sat patiently at the table, waiting for my exoneration or incarceration.

CHRISTMAS WISH
CHAPTER 11

TIME PASSED. A UNIFORMED officer came in with a PowerBar and a bottle of water. My stomach growled, and I thanked him, but he wouldn't meet my gaze.

As if looking at me might make all this truly real.

It was a little over two hours when the door cracked open again, and Captain Romano stepped in, wheeling a portable television with him. He set it up and took the remote before he sat down opposite me.

His cheeks turned rose-red before he finally looked at me. "You apparently knew much more than we did."

He pressed the on button, and a news anchor filled the room with her voice informing viewers of the strange phenomenon that had happened over Manhattan today. Aeriel photographs of the city showed snow and ice creeping out from the epicenter of Central Park, and then that epicenter moved south toward Times Square. Cars stalled out on the roads, and people walking froze in mid step. All the scenes we had observed when we stepped out of the apartment were recorded in real time by satellites traveling in space.

Captain Romano reached over, and grabbed the file folder lying on the cart, and muted the sound on the television. Nervous laughter fell from his lips as he flipped the file open.

"NASA and the Weather Channel confirmed the anomalies." He flipped a series of pictures around so I could see them. "But this is why we are releasing all of you."

I stared at the three-story version of Andrew shooting icicles from his hands. And at the miniature versions of my father and me fending them off while everything else around us were sheets of ice and snow.

"The next clear picture we have is this." He flipped the photo around, which showed New York back to normal and three miniscule figures standing over the broken benches. It was the scene that we'd been initially arrested for.

"So far, we have been able to keep these images out of the hands of the media." He waved his hand over the giant version of Andrew. "For now, but I'm sure it will be leaked at some point. Although the images of the city under what looked like a glacier rolling over it are out there."

He pointed at the television still airing the icy views of the city with time stamps during when we were battling the monster.

"I have to say, I really think this is an elaborate hoax, and when I finally find proof that alludes to that, I'll be at your door with an arrest warrant."

The door to the room opened.

"It isn't a hoax, Captain," my father said as he leaned against the open doorway.

He looked a little worse for wear, but at least his leg was bandaged. Tanya popped up behind him and waved at me with a tired smile.

"Says Santa Claus." Captain Romano scoffed. "Follow me, and I'll get your personal effects."

We followed him to the front desk, and he handed us clear bags with our weapons inside.

"The exit is right there." He indicated a door with an emergency bar across it.

My father gave me a hug and squeezed Tanya's shoulder before he pointed at Captain Romano and said, "Be good!"

Then he turned to me. "See you on Christmas Eve."

His eyes twinkled with mischief as he tapped his nose three times. It was the one signal I knew of his. It signaled it was time to go, and I was sure that was the communication to my mother to bring him home.

Before I could stop him from making a scene, a portal opened, sucking him through it, leaving only twinkling lights that faded after a few seconds.

Captain Romano's eyes widened, just like everyone else's in the vicinity, and there were enough officers around to have witnessed my father's miraculous escape.

"What the..." His gaze jumped to Tanya and me.

I smiled and waved before clasping Tanya's arm and dragging her onto the street and away from the flurry of questions that were bound to be thrown our way. My dad could have done that at any time during our lock up, but he'd chosen the most public place in the station to cement his impression.

I laughed as we stalked toward my apartment. Tanya's ears caused many of the passersby to stop and stare at her. She did glow a little more without her glamour, and both our steps quickened as a result.

"I can't wait to see Ben," Tanya said, and that smile of hers lit up the street.

I didn't know if Ben would still be there based on my conversation with the captain, but I didn't want to burst her bubble yet. I just wanted to get home, put on my pajamas, and eat a gallon of ice cream before we encountered another impossible obstacle.

CHRISTMAS WISH
CHAPTER 12

THE MINUTE I UNLOCKED the door, Tanya burst inside, calling Ben's name.

Yet my apartment was empty. She totally deflated and spun toward me with those big, sad eyes of hers.

"He probably came looking for you. The captain had mentioned him and his partner to me while we were being interrogated. So, I think he may have gone down there at one point."

She pouted. "Why wouldn't he have tried to see me?"

"Because it wasn't their precinct. And they weren't allowed to barge in on the interrogations." I didn't know if I was right or not but I didn't want to jump to conclusions about his state of mind after everything.

But if he didn't show up or call in the next couple of hours, I'd track him down myself. Tanya deserved her happy ending, and I was damned if I wouldn't hand deliver it after what she'd done.

Just as I headed to my bedroom to change into something more comfortable, a knock on the door stalled my step.

Before I could divert toward it, Tanya darted past me and yanked the door open.

Ben stood outside with his hand poised to knock again and his eyes widened at Tanya just before she launched at him, wrapping her arms around his neck as she squealed in delight. His gaze met mine, and after a heartbeat, his arms wrapped around her. He smiled in a way that announced he wasn't so sure what was going to happen now.

I wanted to berate him for his tepid reaction, but the man behind Ben caught my gaze. A jolt skittered through me. My heartbeat spiked at the dark eyes pinned on me, and heat enveloped me. Dimples appeared in his cheeks, and he elbowed Ben.

"Oh. Yeah." He unclasped himself from Tanya and turned toward me. "Chrissy, this is my partner, John Boyer. John, this is the woman who saved all our asses."

"Actually, that was Tanya." I pointed at her and then aimed my smile at John. "But it is a pleasure finally meeting Ben's partner. I was beginning to feel like you were a figment of his imagination."

They stepped inside the apartment, and Ben closed the door behind him with his eyes still glued to Tanya like he was seeing her for the first time and did not know how to react.

John offered me his hand with a smile that could have melted my panties off in a hot minute. "It's nice to meet you as well. Ben has mentioned you a few times over the past couple of years, but I have to say, he way undersold you."

Heat filled my cheeks as I clasped his hand. The world spun, and light filled the room like a prism.

Our hands lingered as if he felt the same magic flowing in the air around us. He squeezed a little tighter, and then our hands dropped to our sides. We stared at each other in a way that screamed he was as aware of what had just happened as I was.

My heart jumped in my chest.

Holy crap.

If I hadn't saved the world, I would have never known this instant connection of souls. The small part of me that had been secretly envious of Tanya rejoiced.

She wasn't the only one who had met her soulmate in this city.

Instead of addressing John's compliment, I focused on Ben and Tanya.

"She went feral after you were frozen. I don't think I have ever seen her that furious at anything. Ever." I tilted my lips in a grin, and I was so glad my voice didn't reflect the tribal beat of my heart or the sudden nerves that bloomed under every inch of my skin.

Ben laughed, but it was not his natural laugh, and I pinned him with a questioning look.

"I. Um." He glanced at Tanya and reached out, tracing her ear with his finger. "How..."

He closed his eyes and balled his fingers into his palm, dropping his hand.

John rolled his eyes. "What he's awkwardly trying to ask is how is this going to work?" He crossed his arms and gave his partner a look meant to scorch.

Tanya recoiled. "What do you mean?"

The squeal in her voice turned frosty.

"I mean the North Pole and New York City. And in case you hadn't noticed, you're an elf. I'm not." Ben studied the patterns on my carpet.

"Anatomically, it doesn't make a difference," I said.

"Her ears," he muttered, avoiding my eyes.

"Are you really that much of a dick?"

His gaze jumped up to mine, and his mouth popped open.

"You are soulmates, you idiot." I reached behind me on the coat rack and pulled off a beanie. "She can wear a beanie while she's here, and you can wear one when you visit up north if you are that freaking shallow."

"Up north?" His voice cracked.

Ben was not handling this well at all. Just like his denial about monsters, it would take a jarring truth to knock the fear out of his heart.

I sighed and traded a glance with John before addressing Ben. "You did not accept monsters at first either." I put my hand up when both he and Tanya opened their mouths. "I know. She isn't a monster. She's an elf. One of the very special ones. She brings the snow." I paused, catching the flash of pain in Tanya's eyes. "Or at least she used to before the monster stole some of her magic, and she smashed her magical scepter to save all of us."

The room lit up.

"Maybe I can do something about that." As the light faded away, my father stood in the center of the room in his traditional Santa outfit with a golden staff that had a green snowflake on the top.

It was different than Tanya's original scepter, but it glowed with the power it held.

Tanya's eyes widened, and both Ben and John stumbled back a step, reaching for their firearms clasped to their hips.

"Easy, boys," my father said, putting his hand out in appeasement.

John was the first to relax, and he traded a look with Ben before glancing my way.

"The powers that be allowed me to craft this for you. But you need to know that if you accept this, your responsibilities will increase, and I cannot have an emotional mess controlling the weather at the North Pole. No more snowstorms in July. Understand?" He tilted the staff in Tanya's direction.

"Will it restore all my magic?"

"It is limited to weather and only available to you for as long as you wear the necklace." He waved his hand, and the staff turned into a magnificent golden necklace with a green snowflake charm hanging from it.

Her frown deepened. "So, no more glamour?"

He shook his head. "Why do you need glamour?"

Tanya met my gaze with pleading eyes.

My focus slashed to Ben. "Ben can't seem to get his stubborn head around dating an elf."

My father slowly turned to him with his eyes narrowed. "He what?"

The air chilled enough to bring goose flesh to my arms.

"Son, you better get your head around it pretty damn quick. You and this girl were made for each other, and powers higher than me made sure you connected against all logical reason. She gave up her magic to save you, so suck it up."

"But her ears," he whispered, like he couldn't unsee them in his head.

My father tilted his head and twirled his finger. Magic filled the space, and before he turned back to Tanya, Ben's ears grew to points like he was a natural elf.

"Dad!"

"They'll return to normal when he finds it in his heart to accept Tanya just as she is. An exquisitely beautiful soul." He straightened his back and offered the necklace to Tanya again, but her wide-eyed stare remained on Ben.

"Tanya." My father's voice cut through her shock, and she stepped toward him but still with reservations.

She paused before she turned to my father. "Is it safe to have this here?"

My father's eyes softened. "We took care of that. Now there's no longer a danger for elves to be in the human realm."

She pulled her hair aside, and my father clasped the necklace around her neck. The air around her charged with electricity. Thunder clapped through the apartment, and then shards of lightning settled into her as if a magical storm had claimed her very essence.

My father stepped away. "Remember to keep your emotions in check. And thank you for helping us take down that demonic parasite."

He squeezed her shoulders, and then air swirled around him. In a blink he was gone.

I turned and handed Ben the beanie. "You might need this for now."

His eyebrows rose, and his fingers scraped over his ear before he darted toward my bathroom. Tanya followed him into the bathroom, and slammed the door shut behind her. The wood did little to stifle their sharp voices.

John smirked and looked at the ground. "Should I expect the same someday?"

He slid his amused gaze to mine.

"What you see is what you get with me. I'm a Kringle." I stretched my arms out. "Besides, who says you'll even be around in another day?"

He laughed, but then his humor faded as he looked toward the bathroom where the hushed voices of Ben and Tanya arguing continued.

"I was a human popsicle for nearly half a day, and I remember every second of it. Time did not stop for me like it seemed to for everyone else in the city. The horror in Ben's face when I became freeze-dried hit something deep inside me. I remember him telling me he knew someone who could help and to hold on." He met my gaze. "He believed in something stronger than the ice entombing me." His shoulder lifted and fell as he waved at me. "He believed in you. And I decided right then that hope was my best bet."

He crossed to the window and stayed quiet for a while. "Hope was the only thing that kept the darkness from claiming me. It tried. It promised me the world and riches beyond my wildest dreams and anything I wanted, if I'd only give into the despair and anger in my heart."

His shoulders flexed. "I'm a man of faith, and I knew that had to be the devil talking in my ear." He glanced over his shoulder at me. "It could have been me out there attacking the three of you if I had given in."

A shiver rippled the muscles on his back.

"I am not wasting the rest of my life on frivolous fears. Not when life can change like that." He snapped his fingers and then focused his gaze on my reflection in the window. "I asked for a miracle, and I got it. I cannot ignore it like he seems to be trying to do."

He pointed at the bathroom where all had gone quiet.

John turned toward me. "And you can't tell me you didn't feel a connection when we shook hands."

My cheeks heated, and I couldn't help the smile that surfaced.

"So, what do I need to know if I date a Kringle?" He crossed his arms.

"I fight monsters."

"I gathered that much from Ben, although I thought you were just pulling his leg and leading him on." His mouth tilted in a lopsided grin.

I licked my lips. "I'm not around on Christmas Eve, and I spend Christmas Day with my family."

"I'm a single cop. I work on one or the other of those two days. And the other day, I spend with my family. Is there any chance of switching off years between our families?"

This man had some negotiation skills. The fact that he was thinking as far as the holidays sent a thrill through me.

"No. I protect Santa on his sleigh ride across the globe. That can't be delegated."

His jaw dropped open. "What do you protect him from?"

"Monsters." I smiled but it quickly faded. "He nearly died this past Christmas, but I was there to bring him back from the brink. My magic is limited to Christmas. Except for Joy. She's my sword."

"The one that turns monsters to glitter?"

I narrowed my gaze and stepped toward him, poking his chest. "You were behind that mirror?"

He grabbed my finger and pulled me close. "Okay, I confess. Seeing you for the first time through that one-way glass was like being hit by lightning." He flashed a grin. "Is that all I need to know about dating you?"

"Pretty much, except, unlike Tanya, I live here. This is my apartment, and I like my independence." Of course, I still needed to figure out how to get my rent taken care of but I wasn't going to voice that right now.

"Good. I actually hate clingy women." He glanced toward the bathroom. "They're awfully quiet."

They were.

"Tanya?" I called out.

The bathroom door opened, and Tanya stuck her head out. Her hair was disheveled enough to give me a clue, and her swollen lips clinched it. Ben stood behind her, and his ears were still pointed, so he hadn't quite accepted his fate of being mated to an elf yet, but he was looking at her with a hunger I had gotten a glimpse of when they first met.

"I think they were kissing," I whispered up at John and sent a wink to Tanya.

She closed the door but not before her determined giggle wafted out.

"I might need a new partner." John looked from the door down at me. "Would you ever consider becoming a police officer and hunting a different kind of monster?"

The notion intrigued me enough to not shoot the idea down immediately. "I can't exactly use the naughty list in a court of law."

His laugh was as magical as Christmas, and he leaned down and pressed his lips to mine.

The universe exploded into a symphony of fireworks. Raw delight filled me from the crown of my head to the tips of my toes, enough to nearly burst through my skin in a rainbow of joy.

My future now had a thousand different possibilities, and I could not wait to see what kind of miracles lay in wait for the four of us.

THE END

Thank you for reading the SILENT NIGTH TRILOGY!

Please consider leaving a review!

ABOUT J.E. TAYLOR

J.E. Taylor is a USA Today bestselling author, a publisher, an editor, a manuscript formatter, a mother, a wife, a business analyst, and a Supernatural fangirl, not necessarily in that order. She first sat down to seriously write in February of 2007 after her daughter asked:

"Mom, if you could do anything, what would you do?"

From that moment on, she hasn't looked back.

In addition to being co-owner of Novel Concept Publishing, Ms. Taylor also moonlights as a Senior Editor of Allegory E-zine, an online venue for Science Fiction, Fantasy and Horror, and co-hosts the popular YouTube talk show Spilling Ink.

She lives in New Hampshire with her husband and during the summer months enjoys her weekends on the shore in southern Maine.

Visit her at www.jetaylor75.com to check out all of her books.